STRAY PAVEMENTS

STRAY PAVEMENTS

SUNNY HODGE

To order additional copies of this book, contact:
Xlibris Corporation
0-800-644-6988
www.xlibrispublishing.co.uk
Orders@xlibrispublishing.co.uk
306200

To those three ink stains behind my ear,
who'll fade and never smear.

FORETHOUGHT

Words that are written to be read usually project with purpose. Words that are written for more self-fulfilling reasons have no end and no moral, they are simply forms of release, and subject to interpretation by all those who happen to take a glance. Like painting a picture, climbing a mountain, or slicing your wrists.

Whatever faith or orientation one follows, it remains a consistent thought throughout generations: 'What would happen if?' In a quasi-educated world that man in his greatness has created, developed, destroyed, and re-built, where constructs are fed to growing cultures and then dismantled within the same hectare of earth, the world I find around me might be very different from yours. Time has allowed man to create deities that govern faith, karma, destiny, and more which determine what we now call civilisation. And have we become more civilised, more educated by disconnecting our links with our previously formed beliefs. By creating and destroying, we find purpose, with or without direction.

In the world I fit in now, over-thinking creates an ugly mind riddled with questions and prejudices. Intelligence is valued but disowned by those who hold it in fear of being so lost in thought that one might sever one's binding in society. Sanity is governed by the majority, and those following different paths are deemed to suffer fame, charity, or disorder. When it comes to sanity and intelligence, there's a proverb that always comes to mind, 'The flame that burns twice as bright, burns half as long' (Lao Tzu).

What if you had been born in a hospital ward across the hallway instead? Would you have the same job, same thinking, or same identity? How often am I conscious of this? And how much of my future is based on my past? Thinking has developed into something monstrous and simply implies that I will depart a different beast from the one which I had entered. Memory can never be trusted, no matter how hard I try. So maybe the best I can do is to list and methodically recreate the path I fell through and try and determine how I once was, a creature untouched by society and thought . . . to decipher the animal I've become.

FRAGMENT 0

This particular family had gone through many households, locations, and residences, much like many others in London. Their first conscious dwelling rested in the suburbs of Essex, where numerous first-generation immigrants resided amongst the plentiful but dwindling cul-de-sacs that surrounded the outskirts of London. The perfect suburban setting, nestled upon the Thames with its grey-green leafy patches and industrial backdrop. Wet and windy winters would layer downtrodden fast food remnants amongst battered pavements, and bleak summers summoned packs of red-skinned workers who swilled beers on warm streets. Perhaps not the ideal grounds for forming families, yet for many, it was a decision made for a better life, lending hopes of stability amongst the hurricane of immigrants strewn across London town. Cultural ghettos littered the entire city: pockets of Indians ruling West Ham, the Africans in Stratford, Jamaicans in Labroke grove, those wealthy Orientals residing in the heart of London, and the Eastern Europeans taking refuge everywhere else—each of them clinging on to a culture innate in them and each as oblivious to their surroundings as the few English natives that remained.

The father of this family, Mr P as he was known to all, was the first to set foot on London's soiled pavements. Fleeing from the civil war that his little island hosted off the Indian coast where he once grew, he left to start a new life in England. He was a man with questionable past and uncertain involvements with a rebel terrorist group that proved problematic to the local government. One certainty was that in London he was safe and free to continue his exploits from afar without interference, sheltering under a business posing to help house legitimate refugees in the United Kingdom. On his tiny island, he led an athletic and academic upbringing, showing great strength and stamina in all sports that were shown to him, and held a promising future in business and finance. Back home, he was a figure looked up to and revered by many, but the years Mr P spent in London had disfigured him, and its lifestyle left his body swollen and his scalp barren. Those few hairs that remained above the shoulder formed webs in large flakes of dead skin, and his trunk of a neck and forearms sprouted black warts. The constraints and legalities that came with his new world visibly took a strain on an elderly Mr P, or perhaps it was all just a mere inevitability of old age. His past faded, forgotten by all, and he lived now as a free and rotted middle-aged man. But if one thing remained intact, it would be that sense of pride for the civilisation he had grown from, an unthinking blind faith in the customs and traditions that seemed obsolete in his current circumstances, yet he still clung on to.

Sister had come from a more gracious background on that island, grown up in a wealthy family with her younger sibling and a plethora of discarded animals all found on sandy copper roads. Their prosperity came from generations before them, inherited by their father, and maintained in shops spread across the isle. The daughters were sent to the best college on the isle, where they led very close and different fates. The younger of the two thrived in classes, excelling in all her academic choices. She became head girl and moved on to attain the highest grades in her year, whereas Sister's interests lay in sport. She donned the nickname of 'Jet' and left college early to compete in national athletic events for her country at only seventeen.

Their strengths paved a way for their future, and the youngest daughter's continued success in education allowed her parents to further her academic interests by sending her to university. Uncertain as to what to do with their eldest daughter, it remained a fact that 'a career cannot be carved from running,' they thought. Even though Sister had always been a 'daddy's girl'—her father followed her athletic interests with pride—on an island where expectations were driven solely towards prosperity, where dreams were folly and liberalism a luxury for women of any age, there was no real or certain future for her. So the decision was made for her to marry into a respectable family, she was told, and it meant her relocation to London. At that tender age, she had no rights or freedoms outside of her parents' interest, and the trust she had maintained in her family was far stronger than her wants. The marriage proceedings were arranged, and Sister was promptly delivered to England. All those she knew and all those she loved were left behind, and her future was paved to follow a man she had only once seen on a weathered copy of a passport picture, till the eventual day of her marriage.

After a few months spent in the capital, her English developed, gaining her a secretarial job in a car showroom. And within a year, she fell pregnant with her first child. Sister didn't love Mr P, or particularly like him. He was the first man she had given herself to, and she knew no different; every act of procreating became a dreaded chore, following the higher cause to extend his family. Mr P dictated her new environment; hence her character remained innocently childlike, her freedoms were stripped, and athletics strictly forbidden.

FRAGMENT 1

Justine birthed from a soil barren to love and warmth, where disciplines created by Mr P formed the root. Sister's mature life commenced with her arrival, and her birth lay fraught with complications. She grew much smaller than other children of her age, tired quickly, and frequently lost her breath. In bleak contrast to her mother, who had always been the picture of fitness, Justine emerged with a defective heart. To be more precise, she had a cardiac shunt, which allowed the bad blood to mix in with the healthy through a small tear in the atrial septum, thus stunting her growth and retarding her physical development. Sister held her closer than anything else in her world, though the early years they had spent together passed in a torrential blur.

On a passing day like many others, Sister came home from work, tending to the family with cooking and cleaning—all the while, Mr P filled his stomach to bursting in front of the ever-glowing television—and tucked her only love to bed. Her husband had demanded tea, knowing all too well that there was no milk to be found in the house. Mundane dilemmas like this could only lead to trouble in such sinister conditions. Thus, he commanded her out, ordering some milk from the local twenty-four-hour shop in town. Sister's fatigued refusal turned an idyllic tyranny into chaos, and Mr P followed her disobedience crudely, punching her belly, then continuing savagely with several more solid thumps to her forehead. Her screams and defences were futile, and young Justine could only listen, lying in bed to wait for the next day when all would be calm again. She awoke the following morning, finding milk in the fridge, though no mother. She searched the house, but nothing. Too frightened to ask Mr P, she ran to the front door thinking perhaps Sister had fled to the neighbours' after all the commotion. And there she saw her laid slumped outside against the front wall of the house, semi-dressed and shivering, with hollowed eyes dark as coal. Sister's face alone gave Justine a sense of the world she was to grow up in. The night Sister had left, forced to get milk after a beating, she sobbed to herself in quiet scorn—shut out of her own house, her body bruised and bathed in the cold night air, alone and defenceless; defenceless was what hurt her the most. And it wasn't the last of abuse that Sister had to undergo, for whether she abided his regime or not, there was inevitably something that made the man furious.

Well-made decisions, I find, are produced by a combination of experience, and one's teaching up till the second that the decision needs to be made. The tragedy in this particular case was that then Justine and Sister knew no better, so they covered up their bruises and life went on.

For almost two more years their world stagnated, right up to the point when Sister's second child was announced. As one can probably assume, its conception was without affection or detail. But in this short period of pregnancy, Sister could lead a relatively blissful life, for nine months at least, till the birth of a baby boy that Mr P labelled Mogul. He developed as a plump and healthy child, a new source of happiness in Sister's small world. But the boy's name had sparked the first altercation since Sister's pregnancy, for she had forever longed to name her first son Didecan, a word denoting joy in native tongue, though her husband had settled on the more traditional name of 'Mogul' for his only boy. That child's first year's living went eerily smooth; he never cried, and never turned down food or rest. Even at eighteen months when the boy contracted an excruciating kidney infection, he reacted in a manner almost devoid of emotion. A speedy combination of antibiotics and steroids made sure he was back to reasonable health, although it remained a mystery as to why he never winced or smiled. And weightier than ever, with a new-found craving for ham induced by the concoction of drugs prescribed to Mogul, he proved to be an exemplary addition to the family and grew well-adjusted to responding to both of his names. Sister and Justine referred to him always as their lovable Didecan, whilst Mr P and legal documentation registered him lawfully as Mogul.

These were steady times for the family, and each member knew their role. Justine, being the eldest, cared for Didecan as she would her own child whilst Sister worked, and both managed the household dutifully around Mr P so that the strains of the family rested squarely on the two women's shoulders, unbeknownst to Mogul and his father. Sister would continue to endure the misfortunes of Mr P; however tender seeds of hostility nurtured restlessness in her—a juvenile life of two children, work, and Mr P couldn't be all. Sister's mind grew stale in the routine that she followed almost religiously day by day, and claustrophobia graciously crept in. It all started with an idea, stashing a little money aside for her interests to slowly accumulate a small sum of cash in her shoes. Without Mr P's knowing, she hoped to one day buy spikes for the track and join the local running club under the guise of working overtime or taking the children to the park.

FRAGMENT 2

A lifetime had gone by since she last stood before a running track; and too much had been interfered with in between. She stood motionless at the starting line, gazing down the length of red asphalt track, hypnotised by the uniformity of it all. Stern and straight white lines merged slightly into one for as far as she could see in those conditions. She remained in a stupor and narrowed her eyes to a slit; it kept the globules of thick rain from blurring her view. Her thoughts were set ablaze as she took in the entirety of the modern running track. It was unlike anywhere she had placed herself before; nonetheless, she sought to find her freedom there. Sister reminisced about her gravel track back home, running barefoot on coarse gravel surfaces with the crippling heat at her back. And there she stood coated in torrid rain, surrounded by the ripe crimson track whose felt green centre carpeted beneath, soft and rubbery underfoot. She was a stranger to the people of the track, and likewise, they all proved anomalies to her too. It was that one passion that brought them together, and it was precisely why she ran so well. Naturally, she was quicker than most of the keep fit members of the club, and she soon caught the sharp attention of the local running coaches who stood at the sidelines. Virgil was one of them, whose sole drive in life still lingered on the track, and at the seasoned age of sixty with two divorces under his belt, all that he had come to trust and respect lay in the rule of the track. It was the one thing that never changed, and it also earned him a steady living as the track coach. He was to have an immeasurable impact on Sister, for her career and her family, but in the meantime, it is for his trust that we credit him.

Sister had proven to be his most promising athlete and friend; her technique and times improved constantly with his help, and the further she developed, the greater she craved the track. He chiselled a small place in his heart for that strange young girl with a curious past and even looked after her two children whilst she ran. He shared stories of the past and spread knowledge of his world around them, whilst spurring Sister on to compete in events around the city. Her popularity at the track sprouted alike her newly adventured independence, but it left her with a lingering shadow of thought that life back home was not at all like that of the other track regulars. Their community made her stronger and introduced her to a deluge of other cultures that lived directly at her side, giving Sister the chance to question the morals of the world she thought she had left behind but still somehow gripped her.

Though if not for Justine, none of Sister's track exploits would be possible. The little girl, though frail of heart and innocent of age, sympathised with her mother so wholeheartedly that she soon took an equal part in caring for Didecan and the duties in the house. By alleviating Sister's responsibilities and allowing her time to run, she could sense her mother's levity trickling down to the others in the confines of Mr P's house. Regardless, she enjoyed caring and couldn't think of any greater pleasure than to look out for her little brother at home or at the track. But the years flew by, and poor Justine weakened. Her body fatigued, and she grew no longer. The daily duties she once performed grew harder, and as days drifted by, her pace of life drew slower. She slept a lot and needed rest after a few minutes of walking; her palm-sized chest tightened and her breathing wheezed forcefully. Full and healthy breaths came but were few and painful. When she first collapsed, Sister rushed her to hospital, holding Didecan, who slept silently nearby. Mr P arrived shortly after work. Justine's eyes looked closed, though her breathing was clearly visible. Thin lips, though pursed, unveiled a constant smile. Sister had never seen her so utterly at ease, so infinitely rested.

After a night's recovery, the outcome was conclusive, a decision left to fate. The doctors reported that her condition had worsened significantly and just two options remained. The first being surgery, an open heart operation to fix the hole in her faulty organ. It promised a healthy life at her current size, if she were to survive the procedure. The second option traced the path already taken, let nature follow its due course, and allow her to live at a declining rhythm, predicting an existence of ten to fifteen more years. The choice was given to her parents, and Mr P chose to appoint Sister with the decision. It was the first choice he had allowed her to make and eternally her hardest, an impossible fate that involved neither logic nor fairness. Then, it was Sister who had the final word.

They took Justine into the operating room that same night. Didecan's first lasting memory came from that moment. In the cold sterile confines of a hospital ward, enveloped in his mother's arms, he slept tensely, saturated in her anguish, sensing her knotted bowels pressed up against his soft temple. I suppose one would call it more of a feeling than a memory, though it wasn't his whilst he rested, joyfully unaware.

After the longest night, just three returned home.

FRAGMENT 3

A whole world misted by routine and tradition became clear at that moment. If the measure of pain is relative and one hurts so much so early in life, does one build a tolerance to it? Or immunity till some greater pain emerges? Even if just until the initial case is forgotten, if that's possible?

At that precise moment, she felt nothing. Just a pressing necessity, a feeling of cagedness, an urge to free herself from the paltry existence she had been smudged into. To Sister's dismay, life still drifted on, and Mr P continued much the same. The house was mournfully still. Resent had laced every interaction; it echoed in every silence, yet somehow, her world continued to creep forth as mechanically and disgracefully as it had done before, even without that integral wheel that once held it all together. Her shadow-drenched eyes sank deep into a sullen face, but it wasn't her face; in every reflection, a deaf portrait stared emptily back at her. Her mind caused it all; she was the cause. It constantly thought—thoughts of possibilities and of escape, thoughts of Justine and of missing, then of nothing. They always ended the same, harsh twinges pickling her heart; then uncontrollable floods streamed down her cheeks and lips. But whilst her mind raced and eyes watered, her emotions remained in a void of feeling. Sister wasn't crying, she was releasing, a slow and undignified letting go, little by little, siphoning her body from the toxins that polluted her. It was all she could do.

One final thought, the final piece, and the process stopped. With haltered heart and muscles taught, Sister walked heavily up the stairs to the bedroom. Each creak from under sordid carpet nagged at her to stop and rethink, to think some more. Her musky bedroom smelt to the very core of Mr P; forever with the curtains of its windows drawn, it filled with dull and yellowed electric light. She left the light off, and gathered her clothes without a noise. Mr P wasn't due back for hours; even so, her every movement flowed with caution and deliberation. She took an empty suitcase and packed it with clothes for a week along with her running shoes that hung, tied to the slats under her bed by the laces. The case clipped up closed with reassuring ease. Creeping to Didecan's cot room next door, she wrapped him up tight in his safety blanket, then against her bosom with her one free arm. On toe tips, she descended those narrow stairs, which let out stunted squeals with the extra weight. She flew out of the house, a free and aimless woman, placed Didecan precariously in the passenger seat of Mr P's rusted black Nissan, and hurled her suitcase into the back. She sat to breathe, and then drove until Mr P's house was but a pixel in the distance.

For less than a week both of them slept in the back seat of his car before Sister found an affordable flat. Mr P would only find her at work, and he confronted her there, pleading with her to come home before an audience of Sister's colleagues. However, her sympathies were exasperated. He hastily retaliated by taking the case to the courts under accusations of kidnapping and demanded legal ownership over Mogul, hoping to repossess whatever respect he had lost. And so the legalities began ...

Sister ran at her hardest in those tough times; it became her therapy, and she craved it more than ever. Virgil still supported her running and her ever-dwindling family, patiently lending the two of them his time and good spirit. He knew all about Sister's strife, and became her trusted friend, for his character was never one to judge, a quality she relished. He had never before been able to push his training regimes so far with any athlete prior to her and, in turn, push any athlete so far. Sister was fine clay with no other faith outside of running, and in a few dedicated months, her talents emerged in hurdling, her times decreased, and her confidence blossomed.

The court hearings were compulsory for both, and it was the first time she had seen Mr P since his scene at work. The case made against her stood for the abduction of Mogul. Sister despised Mr P for what he was and also for what he had done to them. After all the facts had come to light, the ordeal rested solely on Didecan's testimony regarding the cases of abuse his mother suffered. And at such a fragile age, he was impelled to speak out in truth against his father. The final outcome of the hearings declared that Didecan should visit his father on weekends and reside with Sister for the remaining school days. Mr P retorted in outrage, but the court's ruling was final. Adamant to have his own way, he overruled the courts—loitering outside Didecan's nursery on weekdays, aiming to whisk him away before Sister came to pick him up. She always assumed the worst on finding him absent; and feared Mr P would ship him back to the island. Panicked police calls led to strict banning orders on finding Didecan back in that pixel of Mr P's house. Woefully, outside of these flimsy restrictions, nothing more could be done for Sister and her child in a city where the law was still ever so foreign to them. It had become a game for Mr P, and Didecan was the prize, to possess and parade.

FRAGMENT 4

Didecan grew to harbour a hatred of weekends and never spoke to Sister of their reasons for their separation. Her learned opinion of him was kept closely guarded, believing Didecan was a boy to his own will and opinion—an ethos, no doubt, the result of her time spent with Virgil. Weekends for Didecan would inescapably involve either a trip to the temple or a visit to some of Mr Ps' extended family, and both were outcomes Didecan despised. Obligatory temple visits proved an opportunity for him to experience the traditions of that distant and all-so-foreign world that his father spoke of so vehemently. Dazzling kaleidoscopes of colours carved and painted themselves in stories through corridors; they were truly meant to inspire, to set his imagination alight, but he knew that, and it bored him. The other children of his age, tinted like himself, were more compliant to the tales of religious ideals and the attempts at indoctrination that made him swell to bursting. He overheard conversations, distant memories of a language that conjured up the deepest of repulsion in him. In time, he came to detest those noises. After temple, there were classes in speaking, to master the native language, which the other children spoke garrulously amongst themselves. Didecan refused to gain even a simple grasp of what they taught him and silently rejected choruses of word repetition. More often than not, he waited outside on the temple stairs, preferring to sit bored for Mr P to pick him up at the end of the day, once culture school had ended.

Stopovers at Mr P's family would mean making guest appearances at old island folk's houses. They secreted spiced scents and maintained artless pleasantries; their sofas came coated in protective plastic layers, and a barrage of numbing questions would keep him eternally anxious. Absurdities such as 'Mogul, what Tamil words can you say?' or 'Mogul! How are your studies?', and always a 'Why don't you look to do medicine Mogul?' No matter which of the many houses Didecan was taken to, the questions remained the same, the food in every house was the same, and very soon, his response became the same unknowing shrug. What seemed most irritable to innocent Didecan was how wealth-driven these relatives were. In every inquisition, there was a chime for status or the maintenance of it; he felt it sealed in every plastic-wrapped staircase, cling-filmed remote, and in each golden ring that hung off elephant skinned limbs. He dreaded weekend visits from the very Sunday they had ended.

Mr P knew full well Didecan hated weekends and even bought a German shepherd to win him back. 'The dog' didn't quite go as planned, and Didecan used his gift as any child would endure a toy, playing with it when in arms reach, but soon losing interest. Granted 'the dog' made his visits a little more sufferable, but for no longer or any more often. Though for Mr P, she was an uncalculated disaster in the house. She had to be walked and fed; she chewed the wooden ends of furniture and defecated on the carpet. Mr P treated her with a malice only he had perfected, kicking her when she did wrong and locking her in the disused garage until weekends. 'The dog' became uncontrollable and boisterous when let loose; she tore about the house, unruly and wild, tumbling over chairs and stealing food at every opportunity. It only ended when Mr P beat her to tatters, forcing her back inside the garage from where she came. Howls echoed throughout the house, hanging heavily through the hollows of Didecan's mind for days onwards, after all, he was the reason for getting the dog in the first place and for the cruelties that she endured. Each pine and whimper helped him in his understanding of Sister and of why she left. These were times of patience; he sat silent until spoken to. It gave him plenty of rest for his thoughts to gather and a hatred of Mr P to ferment heavy in his belly. And Sister's only response to his protestations remained 'He's your father and you have to see him!'

Didecan's old cot room from all those years back had since been converted into Mr P's office; so he spent every Saturday night alongside Mr P in his master bed, curled around the same corner of the mattress his mother once assumed. Nights were always the hardest part of his visits. He suffered Mr P's snores and grunts throughout, lying awake and thinking of ways to get home, then untangling his plans, to procrastinate on which manner he might be caught.

'I'm going to marry, and I need you to choose whom you want to be your mother.' Mr P opportunely revealed six Polaroids of distinctly similar-looking brown women, each with a lengthy transcript scrawled uniformly along the bottom edge. The pictures were glossy and new, though the women looked to Didecan from another era; they wore shawls similar to the women he saw chanting in temple, devoid of any trace of personality. It was an impossible task since all he saw in those pictures of women were faces of differing ages and shades of brown.

'I have a mother,' he responded hesitantly.

'Mogul, for this house, you need somebody to cook for you!'

'Why . . . I . . .' Didecan feared him and could never bring himself to contradict him directly, especially when left alone. He knew one day he would, he had to, one day.

'Mogul, you must choose for me because you might not like her if I choose for you.'

'I don't know them, I don't want any.' Mr P thrust the pictures in Didecan's incapable hands, ordering him to pick one. In a fluster, he complied and picked one at random. His father seemed satisfied. He had no idea what misfortune he had just endowed on that Polaroid of a woman and again felt anxious for another's impending melancholy.

A month later, he was ceremonially greeted into Mr P's house by a vaguely familiar-looking lady; who welcomed him uncomfortably, adorning him with kisses, caressing his wincing forehead. She introduced herself timidly in broken English as Mr P's wife. Eternally affectionate, she offered an endless array of food and drinks for Didecan each time they met and responded to Mr P's every demand without second thought. Young Didecan just couldn't understand how she could be content under such circumstances, but he liked their simple conversations, even if they did have their polite limitations. With the new lady of the house came the smell of spice and incense, much the same as in those houses he was made to visit. It was a distinctive scent that Didecan was ashamed to carry, so he scurried home every Sunday after visits, threw his clothes into the wash, and headed straight to shower before Sister had a chance to catch him.

FRAGMENT 5

Didecan grew more and more into the features and appearance of his mother, sharing identical skin tone and physique; it was just his glazed look of agedness that reminded Sister of his father. They were often confused for siblings. Sister's careful diet and fitness allowed her to mimic the looks of a girl ten years her junior, until she spoke that is. In just three liberated years, she had matured into a luminous contrast of her former self; all things vulnerable and subservient fell away, and the image that smirked back at her in mirrors was one she felt suited her. Her athletic career took off; she qualified in events all over the country, and her name spread through the running world as a feisty, strong-minded, and somewhat stubborn individual, and one that her peers held in the highest regard. Now that all of her free time became consumed in competing, Didecan spent all of his evenings alongside on the running track, mostly with Virgil, who felt elated in fuelling the young boy's imagination with tales of lost youth and flying fighter planes in the Second World War, of soaring through forgotten skies and escaping enemy territories. Virgil's old age hindered his movement and had eroded his former fitness, but he never tired of learning. He developed a passion for languages and invited Didecan to do the same. Sister could hear their drilling choruses from all ends of the track whilst she ran; it was a tutelage and kindness that no other had patience for, and one of many reasons why Sister stood indebted to him.

The next weekend, Didecan made his usual visit. The aroma of sweet curry leaf swept past him from the moment he approached the cement path; he shuffled up to the front door. An empty feeling came over as he pushed the unlatched door wide open; it wasn't the smell of the room or nerves that seemed the cause, but something in the semblance of the house he had walked into. There was no greeting from the new lady; he couldn't see her anywhere. Mr P expectedly sat distracted by the television and invited Didecan to do the same. This was the usual practice when Mr P decided he was staying indoors, and it bored Didecan rigid. Television had never interested the child, and he grew restless within an hour of its queasy glow; nonetheless, it was the best of the rituals, as weekends went. That troglodyte would sit there for hours, wordlessly sipping cheap cola before returning his son home. It was all he ever drank, and he noticed he was running out. Strangely enough, that time he went to the shops himself to get a couple more litres of the stuff.

Didecan felt antsy on being left alone in Mr P's house; the instant he felt him slam the door shut, the instinct to run free and out the back splintered through his mind. But he restrained himself and took a few calm steps forward to switch off the television. The thought besotted him. How far could he reach if he ran, what path would he take, and where would he hide if Mr P tried to find him? A blur of possibilities ran rampant for milliseconds, but seized as quickly as it spread by soft echoes of sobbing. They trickled gawkishly down from stair tips. Some intrepid reaction began his hesitant ascent upstairs, to the root of the noise. Creeping floorboards muffled the cry of the softened sobs he tenderly pursued, crawling on feet and knees he endeavoured to deafen his footsteps, yet those groans echoing through the house made his skittishness all the more present. 'Mogul?' The ripple sent cold shivers down him, and his little heart raced. He stopped. 'H . . . err . . . Hello?'

'Is he here?'

'No, are you OK?' She was invisible. Lurking in the shadows of the bedrooms upstairs, he felt vulnerable in her presence. After a long guttural sniff, a quick wrist burst out of the darkness and clasped his arm, a hand still damp from tears. Didecan retracted it instantly and tried to shake her free. But again she fell into fits of unstable wailing. He looked down at her, curled at his feet. Clueless adolescent pupils asked her, 'What's wrong?'

'Don't tell him you see me now.'

'What happened?'

'He will beat me!' He was useless; more pressingly, he felt a collaborator in the whole ordeal, a secret witness, and soon perhaps a possible victim to Mr P's brutality. Devoid of knowing what to do or say, they sat in silence for a moment. She regained some composure. He pondered on their relationship thus far and on the circumstances that had brought them to that moment; were they friends who knew nothing of the other outside their weekly confinement? Family? They sat, both perched on the top stair in hallowed quietude till the thunderous fumbling of keys sounded Mr P's return. He found Didecan alone, unflinchingly adhered to the television.

From that day onwards, Mr P's wife led an existence amongst the shade of upstairs, never to be seen elsewhere. But her presence there still lingered. Traces of her loitered in the long black hairs that clung to Didecan's trousers and in the strong scent of food that drifted through the living areas downstairs, and as long as that aroma crept, Didecan was certain she was still nearby. He told no one of the goings-on inside Mr P's house—nobody would understand, and nobody would change it—and decided that Mr P was a force better left to his own and avoided.

In the years that followed, Didecan schemed to whittle down these visits from every weekend, with some excuse or another, to every other. And from that to once a month. Sooner or later, they gradually ceased, and Mr P never tried to contact him again.

FRAGMENT 6

Running took Sister to places she had never known existed, from the extremes of the Americas to the not-so-distant provinces of Europe, with Didecan by her side every stride of the way. The Commonwealth Games were on the cards, and both had plane tickets paid for to Kuala Lumpur. Sister's schedule abroad had been governed strictly by the Athletics Association who bought their tickets and required her to reside in the Athletes' Village for the entire event. After a good deal of haggling, Sister arranged it so that Didecan would be put up in a nearby hotel for the week. His first time solo on an aeroplane was to be by far his most indulgent, promoted to first class as he was too young to travel unsupervised. From the minute he stepped onto the plane till his landing, flight attendants showered him in extravagance. Drinks at no cost, video games, gourmet food at the raise of a hand, but none of it seemed to matter as the flight dragged on and his young body grew restless.

On stepping off the plane, a wall of humidity hit him firm in the lungs, unlike anything he had breathed. Dense air settled heavily in the bowls of his chest. It forced him to think arduously of his own breathing, and he worried how Sister would ever run in those conditions without collapsing. He pushed through the jostling airport, rifling through his pockets for a scrap of paper Sister had left him with the address of his hotel. Absentmindedly, he bumped head to hip into a man who held up a large plastic sign. 'Didecan' was scribbled on the front of it. The uniformed man drove him in a taxi to the hotel where he was to stay, driving past scenes of dark emerald tropics and pristine pavements which lay the grounds for monorail train towers and speedy mopeds, which buzzed recklessly close by—a stark contrast to London's antiquated streets and red concrete walls, but he missed it nonetheless.

They met before absolute opulence, a luxuriant five star hotel in the bustling heart of Kuala Lumpur. Sister was waiting for him at the elegant reception room and hurriedly took him upstairs in the lift to his lodging. They could only talk for a short while before she had to return to the Athletes' Village, and she left Didecan to himself in the room. Dwelling in the solitude of his new abode for hours, he explored all the gadgets that a decadent room as such had to offer. He found objects that he saw no fit use for: miniature safes and trouser presses, and a *mille fois* of tightly wound sheets that prevented him from getting into bed. He made the most of the complimentary hot chocolate, then rifled through the foreign channels on the television, only to re-establish his disinterest. Cautiously opening the minibar, he rummaged through its clinical interior and soon discovered that the costs of each item far surpassed the small change that Sister had left him, resulting in a swift closure of the minibar. The simian child searched every nook of the room, analysing and testing it till boredom. Sudden cramps of imminent hunger plagued him, provoking him to venture out into the unknown. He locked the door behind him and then traced his footsteps back via haughty corridors. Still unfamiliar with hotels and the formalities that surrounded them, he mimicked the porters and settled on a brisk mince through its carpeted hallways, arriving sharply back at the clandestine reception which leaked colder airs to the main road.

The city's thick atmosphere left him asphyxiated; everything that passed by seemed so chaotic and unmanageable or perhaps it was just the air. He decided to follow a familiar path, the rail system, something that Didecan might use without frustration or embarrassment. Like back at home, he assumed that the bigger stations on the map with lots of intersections would almost definitely have places to eat nearby, so he set off to the grandest station he could find.

The monorail was immaculate; he felt that he could have been one of the first to have used the train, it was so clean; stations too were spotless, without a trace of gum or litter. They reminded him of hospitals and showrooms that were never spoilt. On exiting, he found that indeed he was right. Every street corner was beset with little roadside markets loaded with snacks of all sorts and vivid colours; they reminded him of the food that Mr P's wife used to cook. An amount of timidity engulfed him all of a sudden, a feeling evoked, no doubt, by the long spell of muteness that had passed since Sister had left him. Or perhaps it was the almost definite risk that nobody would understand him, even if he did pluck up the courage to blurt out a few meagre words. Barged to and fro by the crowd, the hectic surroundings began to overwhelm little Didecan. He strove to carve a solitary hollow in the bustle, but it proved useless. The commotion of chit-chat echoed unceasingly. Not a single noise permeated his encasement of people, and not one syllable he could recognise. The hurried people bumping past him slowed down to stare, just long enough to catch his attention before marching onwards undeterred—a foreigner once more, tentativeness imbued his every movement. The knee-jerk instinct to run away from the buzz of the main roads and market suffocated him. He ran past waists and sharp elbows into the first quiet alcove he could find. Then silence; in the light of dim flickering lanterns, he slowed to a walk, his heart followed pace, an orange clarity came shortly after. He found himself burrowed in amongst others down a subterranean shopping centre; the atmosphere felt cleaner and easier to take in. Whilst stumbling around, he caught sight of it, just a few metres from where he stood, absentmindedly there, what he'd been searching for all this while. A frozen shore of freshly made sushi devoured him, intricate morsels of silver fish sculpted cleverly before his eyes, just behind a chilled steel counter. Once complete, they lovingly stuffed themselves into the shallow icy crevices that kept themselves wide open in empty excitement for their next neatly packaged bundle of sushi; the tidy production line left Didecan in a stupor. A smartly suited vendor stood aside, rigid and slender. He caught sight of the young urchin's quaint interest and beckoned him forward. Didecan edged closer in trepidation of what form of speech may be required of him, and with all the poise and dignity that seemed fitting of such a responsibility, the vendor craftily packed a selection of sushi into a paper-thin plastic box, then handed it to the boy. Didecan flashed him a thankful smile in return and, in an instant, turned to scurry away, but he was held firm in place by the vendor, who still had his expert grip secured to one side of the flimsy box. The depraved child shot a feeble look back, preparing to let go and run, yet the vendor stood unflinching, staring Didecan blankly in the eye. Steadily, the man unravelled another palm open flat out for Didecan to see. He handed the man all the money Sister had lent him and, before he knew it, received his change.

On his return to the hotel, he thought of the vendor and of their strange wordless interaction, wondering how far he could go on fulfilling his needs as such, with no audible words or common language. Thinking maybe he was incapable of replicating the moment without the vendor, he longed for that man's cunning genius. In his room, each morsel of sushi that he gorged, though slightly warm, felt like velvet capsules down his windpipe. The very substance of dry sticky rice levitated his mood, and each piece of carefully sliced sea creature caressed his belly; before long, his ecstasies slipped him into a deep slumber.

He woke up the next morning to bells, a call from Sister, announcing her arrival in an hour's time. She came early to try and sneak him into the Athletes' Village and bundled half-dressed Didecan into the back of a taxi. Their driver's maniacal driving made sure that they soon emerged on to a vast and barren plain. Multicoloured turrets revealed themselves ahead of them, and in the distance, an oasis of sorts emerged, exempt from the overpopulation of the city. With the taxi still in motion, Sister dropped purple paper money down on to the passenger seat, grabbed her boy by the arm, and hurried him into the fortress, dashing directly to the signposted security station. From what Didecan could work out, it appeared to be the only way in and out of the highly guarded complex. When inside, a sizeable Nigerian man recognised Sister and beckoned the two towards him. The man launched Sister's bags on to a conveyor belt and frisked both of them. With a broad smile, he gestured them forward. Didecan had never imagined The Village to be as epic as the arrangement that unfolded before them, an ecosystem within itself, catering for any aspect of modern life. Shops and restaurants surrounded, providing food and drink to suit the tastes of any nation. Numerous tiers haloed above them, housing rows of luminous facades, which tunnelled out for as far as their eyes could wander. Hand in hand, they tugged each other past spaces containing gyms, swimming pools, cafeterias, and pharmacists. Sister rushed him along to British Team headquarters. It was a particularly musty room, scented with the smell of cold sweat, which formed the meeting point for one of the most multicultural teams in the competition. She introduced Didecan to each team member in the room, knowing that he wouldn't remember any of the names or corresponding event which accompanied their introduction. Sister hoped that one day, possibly, he might recollect those wide smiles that adored her, the faces he had never met before yet felt warm and familiar. In years to come, she trusted that he would look back and picture that odd collection to understand why it was she ran. Didecan felt it was a community that loved his mother, one that wasn't governed by ethnicity, age, or intellect, a team who had committed their lives to what they loved. They quizzed Didecan on his ideas of the city and whether he was all right staying so far away from Sister. One of the athletes offered him a handful of gold-plated Great Britain badges. In his miniature palms, they felt weighty and precious, identical golden gems finished in a gloss of red, white, and blue. They explained to him that those badges were made for each nation and that each athlete participating in the games received five accordingly. A couple of more generous British team members had managed to trade theirs with other competitors to obtain Jamaican and New Zealand badges, which came in their own national colours, and gave them to Didecan.

She dropped Didecan back at his hotel before lunch. Strolling past reception, excitedly he nabbed a napkin from one of the dining tables on his way up, then flitted towards the lift and into his silent den. When the doors were securely double-locked and all was calm, he scampered into bed and smoothed out the napkin. It was to be his canvas, a masterpiece of memories, and his Great Britain badge took its proud position at the centre, leaving an expanse of plain white around it.

For the duration of their trip, Didecan spent his mornings in Sister's company at the village and busied his evenings with excursions to the vendor for dinner. His regular visits to the Athletes' Village allowed him to amass a variety of badges for the napkin. Many were given to him out of kindness, though mostly from the novelty of finding such a stray child wandering through the confines of the Village. Didecan's rapport with the British team grew firmer, and while security got to know his face, they allowed him stay behind little longer to assist in massaging Sister and the other athletes, a skill in high demand and one which he had developed over the years of shadowing her at the track. Word got around fast, and Didecan soon found himself working solidly, massaging the competitors after training; it kept him busy in the morning and proved to be a powerful tool in badge acquisition.

Sister returned to not-so-foreign soils with a silver medal representing a land she would call her own; Didecan returned with his proud mother and napkin by his side.

FRAGMENT 7

By the time Didecan turned twelve, Sister had remarried. Years of running and competing had elevated her name to an almost-celebrity status, and her progress was closely tracked by statisticians worldwide. Mr Meursault was a leading statistician in the field, and an Englishman utterly absorbed in his work. They met for the first time, not unusually, at a track event Sister ran in. Shortly after taking the win, possessed by anxious excitement, he approached her, babbling non-stop of track times and congratulating her on the quick progress she had made. He came across as pale and non-athletic, non-confrontational and prosaic, Didecan never saw him in a temper or a rage, and at times, he reached the extremities of passivity. Mr Meursault had never gone to school and had worked since a child, yet however peculiar his demeanour, his ways remained methodical. Meticulous compulsions allowed him to excel in his work at an age where computers were intangible, devising systems for logging data, running times, throwing distances, names, dates, coaches, lead legs, stride length—anything and everything was filed and noted in a grid of multicolour rows and journals. Mr Meursault, a living encyclopaedia of athletic information, made sure he remained the only person who could decipher his own work. With the use of his infamous green pen, he reached heights of ecstasy; it was a tool precious and limited in its use (the updating of world records); though if misplaced, impending hysteria was guaranteed. It was common knowledge that he was of an odd temperament, but like many of his genius, his work spoke louder than anything.

Sister's disposition had refined with age; she became stubborn to no end, an entity that could not and would not allow herself to be dominated. Whose sound morals encased an emotional claustrophobia that feared losing her new found freedoms, there would be no governing her. Didecan imagined that this was why the couple worked so well together. Sister gained the support of somebody who cared for her and the boy, and she still had the freedom to do as she wished; they never argued because there was never any compromise. Didecan referred to him formally only ever as Mr Meursault; it kept him on his toes and eager to win his stepson's approval. The unfortunate truth was that those bonds between mother and son were so tightly woven that he would always remain Mr Meursault. The couple married quickly and efficiently, signed the relevant documents and made the appropriate agreements, and that was that.

As promptly as they married, they bought a quaint flat in the leafy suburb of West Hampstead; it was small though more than adequate, and like many old houses of its type, it had its fair share of problems while suffering from subsidence and damp. Nevertheless, it formed their very stable haven in a secure and affluent neighbourhood. A suitable location to re-establish a family, sandwiched neatly in between lush cemeteries, trendy boutiques, and bespoke cafes, the majority of which catering for the fast-deteriorating elderly inhabitants who populated that peaceful province, where boys of Didecan's age were not a regular sight.

The inside of the house differed dramatically from the flourish of society outside its brick walls. Junctions between ceiling and walls had grown discoloured by rot, and in passing time, the scent of damp wood saturated the senses of its occupants so heavily that its odour clung to their nostrils as much inside the house as when outside. The wallpaper sprouted decaying wires of varying colours and twisted lengths, whilst carpets remained constantly moist, meaning socks weren't to be worn indoors. The dark feel and physical nature of the house made Didecan believe it had a consciousness of its own. When left alone, he lay flat on the floor in utter darkness and dreamt of floating off to a living forest, where hazy electrical circuits formed a canopy of lifeless crooked branches above him and dank carpeted soils crept into the shoulders of his clothes and hair whilst faint whispers of earthy decay brushed past his nose. Being the youngest, he felt most receptive to the odd temperaments of the house and grew particularly fearful of the kitchen that constituted the chilliest part of the house, an extension that consumed the majority of the small garden behind the house like an unwanted growth. The cold penetrated effortlessly through single-pane windows—simply make-do glass mosaics of differing thickness and cloudy transparency. On the edge of the windows, a one-metre-wide strip of concrete path lay wedged between a head-high timber fence that enforced the perimeter of the garden. Very few light particles succeeded in entering the kitchen, most came from those beams which crept through the larger cracks in the old fence, and the few that managed to spear through the furrowed thicket which protruded above and burrowed down beneath the flimsy construction. What happened on the other side of the fence was a mystery to all, and because Didecan was just that bit too short to peer over from inside, he could forever sense movement from behind. Whether it was a matter of nature or something inexplicable, he avoided being in the kitchen on his own. He felt vulnerable, and every noticeable fidget behind the fence felt like he was being watched. Each twinkle of light that flickered by the edges of his eye caught his imagination; he half expected to spot a pupil staring right back at him through the hollow knots which speckled the entire old timber fence.

The luxury of two incomes coming into the house meant Didecan could be sent to a well-reputed private school nearby. The first week took a lot of adjusting. The teachers and pupils seemed to speak a different language, a refined and confident English, plagued with steely sentiment. He had never encountered as many Caucasians all at once before, and he felt apart both in speech and colour. Children brought gadgets that Didecan only recognised from advertisements. They had it all, but to his surprise, they envied him. He was the only child that arrived and left school unaccompanied; other children of his age were chauffeured to and fro in corporate cars or off-road vehicles, which congested the roads for miles around. They were dropped off by guarding parents and nannies, who held their hands whilst crossing roads and kissed them farewell before they parted. But not Didecan, who walked through town by himself, arriving at school heavily laden like a packhorse.

On his journey home, he stopped off at the Chinese fruit shop, picking up four or five of whatever bizarre fruit took his fancy in the moment. The exotic fruits were always left outside on display and were near frozen in the winter months. He would leave them at home to thaw whilst finishing the local paper round; it took just twenty minutes for him to sprint around the neighbourhood, posting magazines, and he would be back home in a pile of duvet covers, nested upon the carpet, waiting for Sister to return from work. His selection of fruits lay scattered to one side, and his homework for the day was spread out on the floor before him. He scribbled away for hours, with the echoes of television from next door consuming the silence in the empty house before Sister came home for dinner. Mr Meursault would arrive after the two had eaten, and often after they had gone to sleep; hunched over a small desk in the corner of the living room, surrounded by pens and papers, he worked whilst the rest of the household slept.

Didecan did well to stick to his habits; he attained good grades and maintained healthy habits. That independence he wielded so early in life had aged him in many ways and made him somewhat of an

---

anomaly at school. It lent him the makings of a great friend, though he maintained subtle traits of introversion, those of an individual separated from the norm, and so free-willed that he risked unsettling his sense of fitting with the rest of his class. Though one always struggles to find one's place or niche in society, Didecan saw no need to. He was a companion to all, yet nobody knew anything of him outside school boundaries, with the minor exception of one perhaps. Patel was a child who portrayed a youth Didecan had met in many forms before; though this one was a tad more liberal than most. He was from a wealthy Indian family, who dropped him off at school each day in a silver Mercedes, collecting him afterwards in a gargantuan four-by-four; of equivalent expense and grandeur. He didn't smell of spices like the other children Didecan likened him to, though his house did come coated in polythene covers like the rest. He regarded them as a modern Asian family and a picturesque one indeed, led by a dazzling mother and an entrepreneurially balding father, with a guiltless younger sister to keep the balance. They often invited Didecan to their abode for dinner and treated him with the utmost politeness and respect, knowing full well that their generosity couldn't be returned. They represented the best of a culture he had grown to fear and mistrust, encompassing the strength of a close-knit family and reliance that came from it, plus an underlying assurance from all members that if one were to falter, another would assist. That was something Didecan could see the use in, something enviable. Their boy comfortably played the joker of the class, though Didecan knew him better than that. Outside their school's red brick walls, the streets of London were their playground. They explored on bikes, then skateboards, and eventually settled on Rollerblades to credit their idle hours, prowling the filthiest corners of the city until night-time set a curfew on their frolic. The thrill of being out late, getting acquainted with strangers, and making friends on the way was what unified them. In rare moments of rest, they reflected on their runaway adventures—outrunning enraged tramps, dodging dealers, and debating what the boys in the estate behind the railway tracks were doing later.

After a year's worth of pioneering the city, the two of them stumbled upon the finding of a lifetime. One crisp night below the yellow stare of streetlights, the boys discovered a makeshift skatepark behind one of the estates, just down at the bottom of the hill from their school. Crudely built from scrap findings scavenged off roads and rubbish piles nearby, it had been carefully pieced together to create an assault course of obstacles. Filing cabinets formed the foundations of the park, providing noisy surfaces to slide on; rain-softened wooden planks had been placed down bricked steps to make ramps, and a length of scaffold nailed into the tarmac served as an object to grind. This haven gave purpose to their days of street-searching and its discovery brought them even closer. Once a week after school, they indulged themselves in the splendour of the rubbish heap park. Hurriedly, they familiarised themselves with others from the estate who also came to enjoy the pleasures of the park, using an assortment of boards, bicycles, and in-line skates. The boys' earnest curiosity eventually led to their acceptance within the scrap community, and it soon dawned on them that the very youths who used the park with them were once the creators and caretakers of the structure.

The young architects they had befriended possessed totally different lives and interests to themselves; drinking from vodka bottles, they smoked non-stop, and with ever-scabby knuckles, they feared nothing. Money and climate governed their lives. On rare days of sunshine they whiled away their afternoons in a mist of marijuana smoke, discarding their top halves to bask in the sunlight. More often than not, however, when the rain set in and earnings were down, fighting would become the main attraction. There were no etiquettes in these fights besides not taking defeat too personally. The local basketball court served as their coliseum, teeming with bloodthirsty spectators who circled and jeered contenders on, fists raised high within just a few metres of the fight. No hard feelings would linger after, just scrapes and bruises. And every wet week, the two boys limped home, rain-soaked and chaffed, brandishing worn skates in each bloodied hand.

In the rainy winter months that followed, the skatepark endured the worst temperaments of the English weather. The filing cabinets rusted to a thin film in parts, and the rails corroded to a golden brown. The soft wooden slats gradually thickened with woollen moss which slipped sooner than any bearing, and within a month, the park was destroyed and then removed by the local council. The designers had lost their determination to recreate another paradise in the lethargies of marijuana smoke, so the boys moved on, gypsies to the streets, where their skating could progress and evolve into something more than a simple mode of transport. It became something that challenged them, fastening their thoughts before sleep to one growing desire.

Those friendships made on the streets were spurred by a wit and assertiveness that lay inherent in Didecan, but it was the simplicity of popularity that destined him to solitude, and he concluded that divulging matters of his past to friends was an unnecessary pleasure. He was certain that he would undoubtedly be misunderstood, leaving himself pitied, and so in absolute popularity itself he found his seclusion.

Individualism? Isn't it just balance, just like everything else, a happy medium?

Experience leads me to believe simply that an individualistic approach to life is often governed by some insecurity within to gain approval, which by its application would drag oneself right back into the binds of the masses. Would you agree?

By this thinking, surely the only pious individual is the recluse and the outcast. So should it be pariah whom we appoint as the honest individual? The kind so unattached to the formalities and approval of society that their existence can only be formed in relative solitude? Are not the definitive individualists those who are ostracised by society and put aside into institutions and prisons? To be placed on the pedestal of individualism surely most would come to expect confrontation with society's enforcers. What then are the options left for the true individualist? Or is freedom a mere luxury?

Individuals, do they exist in society? Or are meagre attempts to stray from the norm all one is permitted? Where great caution must be exercised so as not to stray too far from the more-comforting expectations in life such as a happy family or a sizeable income—both of which require a certain measure of individualistic prowess—a balance of harnessed insanity remains the only option. So why do I talk to you of this? And what relevance has it? My scheme has been clear from the beginning, whether or not expectations have been met. If indeed I have tailored my enclosure to keep me content, it has always been an over-conscious struggle flickering between the extremes of individualism that keeps me from a shade of serenity, and apart from the uncertain cravings of introversion. Is 'balance' the key, or is it sheer indifference?

FRAGMENT 8

It was strange to think that things wouldn't stay that way forever, but I suppose that's what happens when things move on too placidly. Isn't what makes us as intelligent a species our ability to overcome and adapt to complex problems? There's got to be more than a handful of us who need to create work to remind ourselves of what we are, but I'm going off on a tangent now. Meursault's work impeded more and more on his home life, and after a while, we just got used to not seeing him; he always had some excuse or another. I remember he'd booked a flight to Egypt for one of his track events around that time. Sister picked up a few unusual habits too, like rummaging through his office documents and phone messages while he was in the bath or when he fell asleep. They stopped talking completely and communicated through a tangled tedium, with Sister having to unveil what he'd been up to through his odd scrawls on notes and scribbles on the bits of papers he had discarded in his briefcase. His short stints at home were spent in rearranging and re-sorting the piles of papers and pens which came undone daily. They frolicked like that for months until she found the extra ticket to Egypt. It had been booked for another athlete, a female sprinter she had been introduced to at one of the track meetings once or twice before. She assumed the worst, naturally, and faced him that very night. Mr Meursault may have been a secretive man, but he was no liar. I suppose he loathed confrontation to such an extreme, he

---

lacked the backbone to lie. He admitted all, yet added that he had not been unfaithful. I believed him, and I'm sure mum did too, though if there's one lesson she's taught me which has proved invaluable, is that without trust there's nothing. Her and I are identical in that sense. So she did the smart thing and ended it.

Meursault took it hardest, and admittedly, neither of us had much sympathy for him. It wasn't so much of an issue for me if I'd see him again or not, he was hardly home anyway, and I honestly have no clue about how Sister felt on the matter. I expected her to be angry, or sad even; they were together for a good six years or so. More than anything, it involved a huge change in her lifestyle, but she seemed unfazed. In behaviours like that, I admire her most; there's a lot of coldness in her, and you only get to feel it when you're close. So, very amicably, they sold the house and found two new places to live; Sister and I found a small flat on the borders of North London, and he managed to find a cosy basement studio a little closer to his office. They were both so pleasantly clinical from what I saw of the divorce that it made me think that perhaps the marriage had sprouted from convenience all those years ago, or maybe they were just at an age where it suited their needs and expectations. Either way, the divorce proceedings seemed way too natural.

School was so far away, it meant waking up early and waiting in freezing cold winters for buses and trains that were inevitably late. But I had no choice in the matter; the secondary school was an all-boys school, situated in the heart of the city upon the river and as prestigious as the last. My education was thoughtfully funded by Meursault, who had agreed to manage my education as his part of the divorce settlement, and it was all Sister allowed him to give us.

It intrigued me to see how people split themselves into sects befitting their flourishing and albeit varying traits; it was simplest to see it unfold in the school canteen: smarter kids collected at the edges whilst the footballers pushed in front, sitting predominantly at the centre. The richer boys congregated outside the main gates to dine in restaurants, while the Asian children argued over car magazines and engine capacities in their classrooms eating their home-packed lunches. I managed to float in and out of these social circles without really sticking to one place for too long; though I did share my journey home with the North London lads, who, out of no coincidence, were some of the more mischievous children at school. On train journeys north, we'd take over entire carriages and turn them into our arena. Backpacks worked well for barriers and ties served us well as hand wraps. One by one, contenders squared for battle, where the 'No Face Rule' applied nine times out of ten. Bruises shone through bluest on the paler boys, and washing habits were easy to spot against the white shirts, which were soon reduced to a red mess in a matter of minutes. A lot of these boys were sons of wealthy government officials and politicians, but when it came down to their primal needs and wants, nothing differed between them and the kids from the estate. I found it refreshing, spotting similarities in such separate lifestyles, just unfortunate I could only see it through the constraints of those misted-up thirty-five-minute windows. The train continued, and participants dwindled till only the distant and less fortunate children were left on board with me.

A disparaging difference between that school and my last was wealth and the flamboyance with which it was flaunted by all those who were born of it. It still irritates me to see school children dressed in watches worth more than second-hand cars. They paraded the corridors and stairwells, squealing their worth. I'd never got my head around materialism, and in this environment, I dealt with just about as much as I cared to handle. In morning assemblies boys like myself were paid off by tardy pupils for our seats; if it meant standing for twenty minutes to get myself a decent lunch, I'd see it as their loss. I've never felt that element of worthless prosperity anywhere else, and it puzzles me how those who are given more than what they need will always insist on taking more of what they want. The new environment came as a shock to me; it was a different culture with strange etiquettes and formalities, and on top of that, the bulk of workload expected of us was phenomenal.

I'd cut half the bottom out my tin locker and work it into a hinge to fit my skates, along with the rest of my books. Having to hide it from people passing by was always a pain, but I was to keep the key for more than a year and knew there would be no other like it. I left my skates there the whole day, till school ended; it saved me an extra trip home and back, precious hours till the last tube left central London. Skating in the centre of town was an indulgence most skaters couldn't afford then, not without bunking public transport. Plus it has been, and most probably always will remain, completely illegal to Rollerblade inside the Square Mile. The problem resides in the fact that within this prosperous central Square Mile lay some of the finest concrete-covered streets, marble-sculptured ledges, and perfectly extruded steel rails known to England. Granted that it doesn't seem so irksome to an untrained mind, but in the troubled imaginations of a skater, London Town was their playground, as well as their right. I was fortunate enough to be one of just a few in a carefully handpicked crew who came to know the layout of that Square Mile in even more detail than the very people who marshalled it. When I say 'handpicked crew', I mean to portray a range of individuals from all throes of life, those who had the freedom to skate whenever they wished and the drive to do so whenever they could; most lived off the dole, while others frequented work or college. We varied between the ages of thirteen and thirty and were one of just a few other skate crews who patrolled the inner city's pavements. 'The Capital' was quite likely one of the first and certainly better-founded crews in the Square Mile—elite vagabonds who tore the wild streets of London apart. Armed with camera men on wheels and butane torches for melting wax into virgin grinding material, they created some of the oldest rollerblading spots in London, and we trailed in their wake, skating on the leftovers of their labour. Their ingenuity and abilities are commendable however scandalous their activities may have turned out, for bylaws oozed out from the Square Miles concrete seams and regarded our art as vandalism and public disorder. They wouldn't see it as we did. Taking an object that has been painstakingly overdesigned for a single purpose and putting it to some other use could do no more than merit its maker. We viewed urbanism from a different angle, visualising possible tricks and feasible motions through constructs; a simple set of stairs or handrail could mean a whole day's practice to perfect our skill. It changed the way we thought and how we looked at the world. Mundane train journeys were spent peering out of windows, mapping and scribing potential spots into the pits of our memories, sowing them for the next sunny day. We created a new London for ourselves. Some of our greatest discoveries came from the most obscure urban obstacles, where painstaking conquering allowed one to free something in an object's worth, something that no other were capable of. To put it simply, we were able to warp an object's potential by utilising it in a movement.

Though my sense of direction is terrible, the only reason I've got to know that square mile so well is down to the quantity of time I've spent wandering in that area of the city, be it for school or otherwise. It was an area in such high regard that skaters from every continent came to take advantage of our city, and we'd take them all over. Frequenting murky ledges in locked wine cellars, we could spy the Thames through barred portholes, and just a few arms were thinly nimble enough to permeate through steel bars which kept that spot a secret. Or was it the decadence of the financial districts, set upon polished marble floors and towering glass backdrops? Was it this that they beckoned for? These grounds suited our needs uncompromisingly yet were fiercely guarded, defended by a private militia who proved more ruthless than the gendarmerie. The hostility we faced in the city on an almost daily basis required one to evolve a talent for fast-talk, as the city that birthed me has always been an unrelenting one to live and grow in. The sheer size of it, combined with an integrally cosmopolitan structure, creates breeding grounds for xenophobia. Divisions in rich and poor are so great in expanse yet close in proximity that it makes crime an easy and unnecessary option for many. These effects are only multiplied by the infinite flow of human traffic expunging the city's sense of community, and which, in my lifetime at least, will remain as fragile and temperamental as the much-famed British weather.

Conduct and intelligence were key attributes when it came to selectivity in the crew. I guess you could call it street-smartness; only those who could pick their battles wisely and stand their own, if needed, would be welcomed to the next day's session, envisaging a band of the finest street dwellers.

Genu was one notable individual who loosely met these ideals. A London-born Jamaican of colossal stature, strength, and bravado, he wore a uniform of unkempt tracksuits of the largest proportions and all-weather black puffer jackets to match. His accent beamed, riddled with cockney slang and twisted in modern colloquialisms that just a few of us aspired to fully comprehend. In essence, he was a true personification and inspirer of London's alpha youth, minus all the foolish hip hop facade that often came along with it. We met first one wet weekend, when the crew and I decided to power through the rain and skate the tiled undercover ledges we had found the previous summer. He came from afar, a titan of a man crossing the street towards us; his laddish gait alone drew our attention from skating. He had the confident swagger of a man not to be trifled with. As he approached closer, I felt his gaze squaring each and every one of us up. The crew blew a sigh of relief when he strolled past them and stopped at me. He held a broad and cracked palm out in front of me, I shook it. He claimed to skate, and sensing my disbelief, he demanded we wait for him a while so he could go fetch his roller skates and join us. I half expected him to come back with a knife to rob us, such is London, though to our good fortune, he shot briskly around the corner on skates. After brief introductions, we sessioned the ledge together. His movements when performing tricks were sketchy and forced, and the bulk of his torso counteracted the work of his thick legs. Genu's skating may have lacked finesse; however, sheer brute force didn't permit him to dally on the bigger obstacles.

He became a keen new member of the crew and ventured out with us every week to learn the ins and outs of the city, whilst sagaciously stealing all he needed to survive the days ahead. His gifts in thievery left us utterly besotted, and the few crew members that may have objected to it remained too unaffected to care. It wasn't this transgression which proved to be a problem, but his wild and defiant nature that started to play on the nerves of some of us. Genu's overpowering liberty of speech made his presence forever felt, forcing a couple of the less-authoritative members out of the crew. At first I was unsure as to why Genu took a liking towards me; initially I thought perhaps he could sense in some animalistic way that I was the one who organised the crew, but I later realised that much like him, he had found me a novelty in every way. The boy who had followed a predominantly street education saw me as an opportunity to take a peek into to a system he had been removed from and gain a fuller perspective on the world—such was his nature, a true disciple of 'Darwinism'.

We soon whittled down to just a few strong personalities, those who could stand the harshness of London as well as ourselves. Without a job, money was bound to be an issue, but as Genu had proven, it wasn't necessarily everything. His swift fingers and vast experience couldn't be matched. As he settled more comfortably within the remaining crew, he began to impart trinkets of knowledge upon us, training that was fraught with risk, lessened only by our quick legs and Genu's foreboding build. Our steady morals in the matter of thieving were satiated securely by the conscious decision to steal only from the larger corporations, where the impact was presumably minimal. His creativity in the practice boosted our confidence lesson by lesson. He could waltz into shops looking the obvious culprit, wearing a hollowed-out mountaineering jacket; he was always followed in the least discreet manner by cameras and security alike. They caught his every movement and still he managed to emerge unscathed with a bottle of Veuve Clicquot up his sleeve or a twelve-inch pizza down the abyss that was his trousers. Of course, his wayward appearance made things trickier, but the nimbleness with which he was endowed far outweighed that trifle and made us feel at a natural advantage to adapt and improve.

Our first tutorial began in the sneaky placement of drinks cans and chocolate bars in our open skates, keeping one eye on the aim of security cameras all the while. We progressed rapidly to larger streamlined objects that were simpler to sleeve. Deodorant cans and small baguettes were perfect; they were smooth and frictionlessly sunk into the natural contours of our baggy clothing. Moving forward, we turned to bulkier sandwich boxes and noisier items such as crisps; instinctively we learnt to conceal them down the waistband of our tracksuit bottoms and let them settle at our ankles. People rarely looked down, and if you're on the opposite side of a counter, there's no stopping you. He explained how the alarm systems worked in shops and how to make objects disappear within metres of someone watching you. It was all misguidance, knowing how others think and what they can see from a distance. The real skill was in interpretation and making quick judgement on one's environment; it had nothing to do with the object itself, but with everything else that surrounded—well, that's how he described it.

In the early years that we spent patrolling London's dark innards, we had stumbled on to more than our fair share of illicit encounters. The more often I think back to it, the more I realise how fortunate we were to have slipped and slid our way out of trouble, constantly learning and improving every day. Yet with learning one doubtlessly makes mistakes, one has to; unfortunately it was the harsher ones that stood to curb our youthful recklessness. After years of teasing the parameters of a faceless society, one got a little disorientated, and we soon lost our perspective on who we were and what we were capable of. In my meagre defence, I was but a bystander in this menial event, but if there's one thing I've taken from hindsight, it's that to be a witness to a wrong is to be as good as any perpetrator if you do nothing in your power to help.

It happened by St Paul's Cathedral one crisp night. We were practising on the stairs in the courtyard; the climate around the central walkway at that time of night felt like a dream, the warmth and colour of the insides of eyelids. Hazy orange street lights illuminated our way, cut neatly by turgid silhouettes, reflections of rigid lamp posts that striped the stairs. If it were not for the biting cold, we would all have been sent to sleep. In daytime, the area was a hive for commuters and tourists tearing up and down the path like worker ants in the height of summer, but when the day drew to a close and shade trickled down the icy steps, the courtyard fell dormant to lovesick couples wrapped up to the chin in scarves and Christmas jumpers; they sat and watched us hand in hand. If we could call the streets our home, the crew would be our family, and like in many families, I'm told, disputes erupted from the smallest of catalysts. In this case it was Genu, who locked horns with another long-standing member of the crew JL—a proud and plump Caribbean lad possessing a mouth as verbose as a machine gun, holding talents both in music and the rhythms of skating. The details of what sparked their exchange are trivial and the outcome a little more stifling than we expected, for Genu's lackadaisical responses to his opponent's taunts resulted in JL, without shame or subtlety, shattering a street sign nearby and then threatening the giant with the broken pieces. It wasn't often that disputes rose to this level of animalism, and the fact that we allowed it to escalate was an offence we all felt guilty of. We watched a while, expecting the fuels of the altercation to run dry. Then all stood still. Turned to stone, we heard an echo at first; the faint yelps were indistinguishable but felt closer in seconds. Vacant barking bounced through nightmarish avenues. The streets were now empty, and we felt those howls reverberating on our cheeks, vibrations that thoroughly doused the testosterone-fuelled flames.

Knowing that the consequences of our actions were ever—encroaching, we swiftly hurried our belongings together to make a quick escape on skates. Patel and JL being plump and firm of mouth stayed put, whilst the rest of us split at the sight of charging dogs and police. Genu took off separately, knowing that if caught, he'd have much more to account for than a street brawl. So he fled to the depths of the underground, hoping to take the first train to safety. The rest of us sank into a thick maze of commercial towers nearby. We weaved in and out of the capillaried streets endeavouring to lose them, fleeing in every direction but those of the barks which rattled up through old brick buildings. Our fitness wavered; a hidden alcove we ran past would prove perfect to change back into shoes and regain our energies. Hoping to be less conspicuous, we sheltered in the dark, behind a rancid set of overflowing wheelie bins, sitting motionless, waiting. The barking grew louder, and crisper. In seconds, we were surrounded, then cuffed, then hastily thrown into the back of a riot van for further questioning.

None of us saw a friendly face till our release the following morning, and abiding by our code of honour not one of us felt compelled to tell anything of what took place the previous night. As for Patel and JL, who stood their ground, well the police had accosted them at the scene of the crime, and they were told to stay put in order to better pursue us. Left unaccompanied, without a second thought, they sauntered off at a leisurely pace to safety. We the incarcerated were strip-searched and drug-tested, and our laces confiscated so we couldn't hang ourselves in our cells. They were brightly lit, too bright to sleep, and cold. Mine had a single sterile toilet stationed in the corner, and it was about the only item of furniture I was permitted. I couldn't contain my anxiety any further and explored each intricacy of the cell, committing every etched detail and erroneous graffiti to memory, thinking that I could be dragged out any moment; after all, I had done nothing wrong. I began to lose all sense of how long I had been in there. Sifting through past thoughts became my only tool of measuring time; without natural light or a watch, I had to use each consideration as a landmark through recent history. It became even trickier when I contemplated on which thought, of an endless list of thoughts, had been my most recent calculation of how long I'd been in there for. I'm sure we each invented our ways to busy ourselves in our respective containers. I whiled away the rest of the night wide awake, bored, and unrested, with just a polystyrene cup to channel my frustrations on. Unskilfully I engraved it with fingernails to a chalice of the greatest design, but then overused it to shreds. They released me with no lasting record at five the following morning, and my watch and shoe laces too.

We weren't always so fortunate. Our entanglements were never an exact science and so often ended in bloodshed. My first real scrap, if you could call it that, occurred in one of the all-encompassing estates that tormented West London. A light drizzle hung high that night, almost suspended in fog. It soothed JL and me on our weary limp home. It'd been a hard skate at the only weather-protected skatepark in town, and as usual, we took our short cut to the station through gaps in a grid of parked cars. Our limbs ached, oozing lactic, and the parts of our bodies we gave the least concern to would sporadically grip with cramp. Our weighty bags felt cumbersome, filled to bursting with skates and tools which never granted us enough room for extra clothing in the winter months, so our arms and fingertips froze stiff.

We must have appeared as vulnerable as we felt. And one man was all it took. A gym-fit African fella, dressed entirely in black, he had a single broad and silver chain lassoed around his neck; it hung neatly off his shoulders to exemplify his top heavy build. He pushed through the two of us, rolling his two shoulders in time with his hips. Two protruding lips demanded a phone, just one, from either one of us. An attempt to divide and conquer I figured. JL made a swift sprint for the station, leaving me stationary. I stood wavering, and in fearful clarity, I took a step backwards but the aggressor mimicked with a pace forward in my direction. I stood alone with the man—he who held his fists ready and clenched and whose dry, hooded forehead floated in line with mine. He toppled me to the ground like a leaf, forcing his spread palm across my chest to keep me down. Struggling free was futile, and I could see no way out of it with all my belongings, not without a fight, and by the looks of it, a losing one at that. He barked another terrifying order directly into my head, saliva sprinkling my brow. Did I sense a little Nigerian twang in his tone? Half-minded I'd demanded to keep my SIM card. Bravery? He smirked before lifting his chain with both thick fists, releasing a hefty chuckle as he did, purposefully ravelling it around lighter brown knuckles. Then he sharply ploughed it into my impressionable jaw; my left cheek swelled to disproportion, bleeding a little to the thumping of my heart. I lost a phone that night and, more significantly, my pride. The journey home was lonesome and resentful. I wouldn't permit it to happen again, I told myself that and I was sure of it.

When it came to choosing places to skate, race would always be a factor. BNP promoters littered better-founded estates, and minorities risked both torment and injustice. We had a fairly good idea of the safer estates to skate, depending on the mix which formed our crew that day. I look back to one night the three of us spent skating beside the aged HMS *Belfast*. It docked permanently along the river bank that neighboured London Bridge, and our location was one of the few safe and self-secured financial districts south of the river. Wealth was rife when you stood over the narrow grey slate tiles of the More London Estate, yet just a stone's throw further south harvested a multitude of council blocks, many of which were infested by BNP-affiliated residents and gangs. We weren't exactly the types to shy away from those parts of our city, but we were not so foolish as to lower our guard when skating nearby. We'd managed to befriend a handful of security guards who patrolled the glass towers and struck a deal with them concerning skating on their territory. On clearer nights, myself, Genu, and an individual who went by the name of Py would skate the estate till the morning hours. Py was a Jamaican through and through. Arriving in England at the age of fifteen, he was thrown into a system of foster care with no permanent home or family. His fluctuating temperament meant his foster parents changed on an almost monthly basis, as did his principles. In the three years I got to know him, I saw him entangled in the confines of fundamentalism as an atheist and in Islam; then he finally settled with Christianity. He hadn't a penny or an ounce of logic to his name, but he remained a committed skater who knew the streets and kept his place firmly in the crew.

We basked in the light of the river on rare nights like that; the moon's crisp beam shone brilliantly upon the Thames, a pale luminosity diffused across our path, leaving our vision no finer than a comforting violet haze. Eager tourists dotted the landscape, capturing London's glimmering attractions forever in time. These moments were blissful, and unlike many urbanites, we took the time to take in the city at its most splendid ephemeral state, irresponsibly placing those images into our cached memories to smudge and blur with age. Our session at the chubby guard rail that we aptly referred to as 'fat black' had reached its peak, and the river shone at its brightest. Our quiet was but short-lived, and it came toppling down alongside a speedy barrage of stones that hurtled towards us, most of which ending their trajectory at Genu's gigantic feet. Slurred taunts followed. '. . . fucking niggers . . .' and 'Piss off, you Paki' was about all we could make out. Our eyes settled naturally upon a gang of fifteen or so youths draped in football shirts, wielding shaven heads and some with wooden sticks, while others hurtled rocks and other loose objects found along their way. Before Py or I had time to react, Genu raged, 'Your mum's a blood claat African!' Not the wittiest retort considering how far outnumbered we were. Genu appeared exhilarated by the conflict. They marched ever closer, and he remained defiant. Looking backwards at the path towards the station, I spied Py's outline a good fifty metres away. He appeared to be on the phone, I could only assume, to the police. Genu glared at me. I could feel his restless heat, a wide grin spread across his capacious jaw. My own eyes were wide and tentative. He ordered me to leave, knowing that I'd stay. When the gang were within just a few metres of us, he had the primitive whim to place his skate around his sturdiest fist and charge directly at them. I stayed. Adrenaline seethed to the very tips of my fingers at the sight; that infernal soldier chased them back up the path they came from. They ran so far that I lost sight of them. I remained so attentive that all I heard came from deep inside my pounding chest, I heed the cool river winds that spiralled through my thin hair, and from afar, I spotted a black mass running towards me, frantic and disjointed, shortly followed by a flock of white. Sense came flooding back to me all of a sudden; I picked up the remaining bags, threw Genu a gesture to meet at the station, and all three of us were separate.

It was a tiresome burst to the station, hindered by the weight of our bags and the buzz of traffic whose tail lights obscured all vision through my condensed breaths. Nearer the station, we met again and spotted Py loitering behind train barriers. We darted in his direction and leapt over turnstiles to join him. In moments, two stern ticket inspectors attempted to detain us, but the gang fast on our heels caught up, jeering and spitting though the gates, quickly turning on the two guards too, who fell in their path of carnage. The more mischievous attackers clambered to the tops of the barriers, only to meet a brisk jab or a kick from Genu or the ticket inspectors. Their frustrations grew and insults distorted to hurls of spittle which rained above us, until an indistinct wail dispersed the crowd and the riotous storm came to an abrupt calm. Genu was the last to run into the dwellings of the station as the authorities arrived, escaping in the hurricane of confusion and yelling that the police would always bring with them. They ordered that we drop our bags and kneel, hands above heads; promptly we were pinned against a wall and searched. For just a second we struggled free, before the full strength of the law was forced upon us. The two of us were floored and cuffed. Steely polished marble shook through the coldest length of my face, vibrating with every train that set off below us. I tried in vain to withdraw the globules of lukewarm saliva that drifted to the tiled floor, but my twisted arm rested under the manipulation of a brute more than twice my weight. Several trains sped by before the situation was resolved; a mere miscommunication was all they reported. The gang ran free, and police left us addled at the station with a gratuitous apology and a fond farewell.

FRAGMENT 9

I'm gifted with the unsavoury habit of savouring the moment. The years that passed by have been quick and full; lessons were learnt daily, and mistakes were numerous and affordable. Those times were happy years for me; I knew that then, but then what's the use in knowing that now?

At seventeen, I moved out of Sister's and into a small boxroom in Camden Town, sharing it with two working women who kept themselves to themselves. I managed to find this part-time job in a busy little sandwich shop on Tottenham Court Road to pay the rent just before university was set to start. Surprisingly, exams at school went pretty smoothly considering the goings-on outside, and I'd acquired myself a position at a decent university. Mum seemed to have made a little more out of it than perhaps she should have done, saying it was one of the best in the city, for my chosen subject that is. In the mania of exams and not having a clue what to do with myself, I chose Mechanical Engineering because it sounded tough; it's a notion I'd brought about to test myself. Call it self-inflicting or ambition, I reckon it all boils down the same.

I exalt Camden and everything that it stands for—it is freedom; it's a breeding ground for individualism. I could walk out my front door stark naked and nobody would bat an eyelid. Granted, outside of the little market stalls and tattoo parlours it lacks a sense of homeliness, but for most in London, whose families are oceans away, it serves a purpose. Down a bright and buzzing basement, Chuck Berry played on repeat, from 'Guitar Boogie' to 'Deep Feeling', back to back for hours on end, three painful hours to be exact. In that pit, I sought to eternalise a feeling in ink, the stencil of a grey langur pin pricked across my back, a symbol of de-evolution, simpleness of mind—happiness I mean to say.

Out of no moral obligation, I also made the decision to stop stealing. It had become second nature to all of us, and still nothing bad had come of it; it felt like the more we did it, the better we got at it and I worried that it could get out of hand, or that it'd be too tough to give up. I couldn't rely on it for much longer and definitely didn't want to be doing it into old age, so what better time to kick it than the present?

Is it strange that I come to be disappointed by expectations of karma? The idea of 'what goes around comes around' seems to make some kind of sense, even if I realise logically that it's all superstition. That said, by giving up actions which have negative connotations in society, one expects injustices to be no longer burdened on them. I realise the concepts of good and bad are relative, so does that make karma subjective? I've found that the most fitting definition of a good action is one that doesn't hurt another or oneself, simple. Nonetheless, the idea of karma is a much-romanticised ideal and one which is not supported by logic and, as I was soon to find out, experience.

The crew started to mature, and so did our interests. Suddenly, women and work took over, confining our skating to weekends. We all still skated, but times where we were all out together spread fewer and further apart, and those who had the will to skate outside of their changing lives began to tag along with the more regular crews. In those separated times, one stray character, whom we dubbed 'Portuguese John', led me to an unfortunate fate. His grasp of English was limited, so he communicated best through his skating. We Londoners knew nothing in the way of Portuguese but were more than happy to show him the ropes; we finished up early that day to end our session at the pub, which was another thing that happened more often those days and was a social activity Portuguese John avoided at all costs. The afternoon I speak of rested squarely in that scorching hot and sticky week that comes but once a year in London, summer as we like to call it. It brought sorts out their houses I'd only ever see in that one week and was as good an excuse as any to wear those scratched sunglasses you'd bought the same time last year, and stroll around the city in sandals. A day like that couldn't be wasted inside the pub, so the two of us split apart from the group. We headed to Peckham library, where we could skate a perfectly positioned handrail in the sweltering plaza. A sunburnt audience joined us, fluctuating in mass depending on how hard we skated or how badly we fell. I detest crowds, even more so photographers. They're fickle; your greatest admirers when landing tricks and are quick to make friends and conversation. But if you fall (a vital part of progression, I may add), you're but a jester to them, a source of slapstick amusement, and one never gets used to being laughed at, especially when twinned with the very pain that provoked their cruel smirks. Nonetheless, we skated forth for most of the day. The light started to fade and intermittent evening showers began to wave us by; they moistened the concrete tiles below us and made our wheels slip at every push and turn. So we packed up, and the crowd soon washed away. Showers turned to warm rain, and the streets lay almost bare apart from small pockets of commuters who deposited themselves under bus stops and shop entrances. We skaters didn't care much for the rain, though when on foot it didn't bother me too much. I'll never understand why people waste their time avoiding the irrevocability of getting wet, taking refuge under trees and umbrellas; what's the point? We cut right through it, across the bleak plaza to the bus stop, marching through the heaviest torrents, which spurted waterfalls off our noses and chins and bled the dirt clean that clung to our blackened palms. Our bus stop overflowed with commuters avoiding the downpour, and the two of us waited beside it in the rain.

I could sit and watch the rivers for hours, the ones that build up at the sides of roads that carry away cigarette packets and empty cans. They're ever so shallow, mind you, that the smallest pebble could knock a litter boat astray. Cigarette butts gather together in islands and petrol streaks rainbow their way, tinted freckles, ever-changing and tragic. Some sticks fell short, whilst others sped through; it's impossible to predict. Two boys affronted us, their description and shape lay hidden behind thick hooded tracksuits, their voices distorted by the heavy rain. It was clear they had some interest in John, as they asked him in muffled tones for the time, over and over again. Unable to fathom their urgency, he took his worn phone out and found it promptly pried from his moist grip. Casually the hooded assailants sauntered off without a care. Tin drum raindrops diluted John's cries for justice and fell bluntly on the crowd of bystanders at the bus stop. They watched on. Unmoving and able men, there were many. Had I joined them? To look on was far simpler. Whether a friend or otherwise, shouldn't somebody help the man?

I took after them, hoping to tackle one to the pavement; he went down in a spray. The other stirred, attempting to grapple me in a headlock, but the rain played in my favour. With desperate tearing of long sleeves, my slippery arms were untangled from their grip. The phone flipped free in the tussle. I briskly pocketed it and ran loose. It was a short brawl, and one I may have won, but the boys ran off in the opposite direction, leaving me with the ripped remains of a sordid jacket. It fell flimsily off both shoulders, and the cool drizzle subdued heavy throbbing veins. Portuguese John thanked me with the few English words he could muster and took his leave on a bus south.

The people at the bus stop, they watched me; I reflected an indirect glance back, but their stares were remote, unchanging. I was but a source of continued amusement to them. My bus was on the way. I could see it creeping from the distance at the peak of the hill, and the crowd began to shift restlessly. A servile mass whirred and nudged itself forward into a disorderly queue, and occasional fits of elbowing followed, all under a general din of complacency. I made my way to the back of the rabble but was pushed past and obstructed by those two same hooded boys, plus another. Their new accomplice ravaged me with questions, expelling them in quick succession. 'What 'enz u from?' Refusing to respond, I barged past him, and the three of them parried by dragging me to the pavement once more. Escape had to be on the bus. For the second time, I slid free of their rabid clasp and forced myself into the safekeeping of the bus. But my open doorway was full, congested by the crowd who looked on sheepishly whilst retiring to safety. Petulantly I squeezed past, pushing through a thicket of hips and swinging handbags. I looked back to catch my pursuers and caught a wisp of smoke spiralling through wet air, after hearing three crisp hydraulic thuds bounding off metallic tin walls. Flashing my ticket to the driver, I stumbled on, the doors closed shut, and we proceeded off to safety.

I took a few feeble steps forward, fearing to look any further, knowing the entire crowd's eyes would be set upon me. Warm free-flowing liquid spilt down one side of my jaw, leaking gracefully to the easy-wipe lino floor. My head felt numb, and the rush of blood failed to slow. Looking up, totally silent, I was engulfed in yellowed whites of eyes, their mouths glaring, wide as their pupils, and neither blinking. They cleared a path for me to stagger down, and a neat space was made for me to squat near the exit. My journey down the length of the bus seemed double, giving me time to find the root of the bleeding. A warm sphere disclosed in my jaw, very much hotter than the layers of skin that enveloped. It left the surrounding area singed and in a tingle. Motionless, it sat obstructed by the bone forming my lower jaw. I squeezed at it, instinctively, at the end of its trajectory, pinching it through tunnels of hot flesh back out the way it had entered. A mass of lead slipped free out of bloodied fingers, hitting the deck and making an inert metal thump as it dropped; then it rolled away out of sight with the rapid swerving of the bus. Sudden movement overpowered my coordination, leaving me vulnerable to its every turn. Struggling to find my way, I sat upright with my back flat against the doors. The crowd's unwavering looks followed me throughout. 'You should go hospital, boy,' an elderly Patwa-sounding woman blurted. I gestured that I was fine. 'Dem boys sure did you good. You shouldn't mess around with head trauma, could drop down dead any second now, don't know!' I took a better look at the belated Samaritan. Small and withered, she stood above me with a puckered face and bulging eyes. Her pickled limbs were propped up by a tartan shopping trolley; she looked to be covered by a wardrobe's worth of winter clothes layered one over the other. I was still crouching as velvet-streaked palms cradled a bleeding bulge behind my head. Clumsy fingertips explored the crater tucked under tufts of matted jet-black hair. It felt swollen and damp to touch. The old Jamaican lady's paranoia, the attention—it was unbearable, and I toppled out on to the pavement at the next stop to call an ambulance.

The cold blew straight through, accumulating inside me with every minute that passed. I hate nuisances as much as hospitals, and needles and all the paraphernalia that comes with them. Upon the concrete I leant against a crumbling mossy brick wall, thinking of the possible outcomes that lay in store for me; none filled me with enthusiasm. Heat was in abundance. I could see it surrounding me, but it was of no use for it wouldn't sink in any further than the very skin that protected me. Ears and fingers, then hands made everything they touched cold. Cooling palms gripped tight against the hole, kept it at bay till they came.

I was sped to hospital. I despise them; they're sterile and cold, unforgiving and uncaring, reeking of illness and delayed death. They left me to the X-ray; then I was operated on an unsteady bed.

Some foreign body had to be removed, they had informed me. I was to be put under local anaesthetic for this simple procedure. In three dry and prickly strokes, a patch of hair surrounding the crater was skilfully shaven; taut bulbous skin felt punctured and anaesthetised. Three separate injections around the primary wound were introduced till my head felt like glass. Flickered reflections from a well-polished silver tray darted past my eye line; a scalpel was removed and then put to work out of sight. It commenced with sounds of scraping, irate screeches induced by the fumbling of a stainless steel blade teasing at the stubborn ball bearing dislodged within me. Those scratches I heard were not with my ears but were produced through my entire skull; my cranium turned into some archaic musical instrument. Each tender scratch left me wincing till an impromptu metallic pin drop chimed the end; the object had been successfully spat out on to the steel collection tray, along with a nest of scalp shavings. They bandaged me up and handed me to the police for further questioning. The firearm was identified by the projectile, a gas-propelled hunting pistol used in hunting for killing rabbits and other similar rodents. The three boys were apprehended and tried for acts of grievous bodily harm, and the gunman for attempted murder. And within a month, they were let back on the streets.

On occasion, I feel that instances such as these are necessary misfortunes; they help put things in order, perspective even. Sister used to say, 'Whatever doesn't kill you, only makes you stronger.' Whether she believed it or not is a different matter.

I heard screams. Sister's; they sounded like mum's, filled with anguish. Peeling the warm duvet off my back, I step out and focus on the screams. Running through bright yellowed wallpaper, through a windpipe of corridor to her bedroom. It's further than before, so far that the soles of my feet begin to throb. The screaming stops, and I'm left standing in the room; its dark and lazy vision scatters with light purple sprinkles. Mr P's bloated outline stands over Sister. His smell engulfs me . . . musky damp spice makes my eyes water, transports me backwards in time. Once connected, I fight the feeling, and forget. Not a word. I can hear my chest breathing; it's all the three of us can hear, heavy and controlled. Sister's on the floor, her tears restrained under swollen eyes, stagnant. They hold their own weight. In unison, the interstices that fill my lungs seep with heat, breathing loses rhythm, a beat is missed, and he darts past me.

In the kitchen, I'm exposed by dawn and a blush of sun that illuminates the cold extension. The air here is sliced by fresh and indiscriminately cold light. Still, faint traces of his stench linger. He's hiding behind the fridge, cowering over the old wicker basket bin. I can spy his flaking elbows tucked tight against his bulging stomach, both of them poking out grotesque in front of me. He remains motionless, and deadly silent.

In my right hand, I grip a black handle; it extends comfortably to a blade of sleek and nimble proportions. In length, it extrudes no longer than my forearm, and it's width begins at just half an inch at the base. The beauty of the sinister device I hold comes not solely from astounding elegance, but from its malformation. A single small and precious dimple, blunted at the tip, the embodiment of my tool's vulnerable innards. I'd only ever used it for cutting vegetables, but in my ready hand it gives me purpose. Deep inside my chest, a cavity constrained and boiling with anger churns, wrenching tight at the muscles down the cores of my forearms to the clench of my fingertips. The tension in my bicep holds no more. Teeth tight, I approach.

His thick palms propel towards me, pushed out by brutish arms, in vain. The first incision went straight for the stomach. The next stroke was mine, an easier one, and through the ribcage I delivered true. One after another, they slipped in with little resistance. Once his leathery skin punctured, the full length of the blade slid in smoothly, and the hilt was all that prevented my entire fist from penetrating him.

The initial fury's subsided. I feel at ease now, soothed. It's a welcome relief, and every stab forth lets a little anger out. Just a little bit more, and I'll be rid of it.

My eyes spring open. It's dark, and I can just about separate the faint outlines of snaking wires that protrude from wicked walls. I'm breathless and warm, and as reality unfolds, I find myself in bed, staring upwards. I know it wasn't real; I can comfort myself with that thought. Relaxed feelings linger, and my heart slows softly to a comfortable pace. This cosy feeling of contentment makes my body hairs protrude, scratching the bed sheets. I'll have to try, try one more time to drift back once more.

FRAGMENT 10

When the weekends started to get wet and murky, I joined a young crew from East London and took them one week to a sheltered spot tucked away under a flyover. Our ledges were covered and cascaded in tiers of large tiled platforms to the ground like a dried concrete valley, descending to a tiny crevice of a footpath which ran straight through the middle. We were perfectly secluded and, more importantly, dry. We took it in turns to explore the area for hidden architecture and then return to the amphitheatre-style ledges to finish up.

Our legs started to go into spasms, and we decided to pack up. I remember holding my phone between ear and shoulder, mid-conversation, and tying up my laces all at once. A group of passers-by from the footpath jogged over to talk with the rest of the crew. I observed the two groups covertly through my phone call; it was the two taller lads who spoke, one looked as if he'd been in a scrap, with his arm encased in a pink cast. The three younger ones followed their lead, distancing themselves and keeping constantly busied like timid foxes. They scanned their surroundings and occasionally delivered whispered messages to one another with ever shifting eyes. The older ones momentarily lost interest in the others and minced stealthily towards me. The injured one interjected, questioning me on the model of my phone. I knew what I'd have to ready myself for, though in the blink of an eye my phone was snatched off me. I had but one shoe fully tied; nonetheless, I threw myself at him, hurling the scoundrel to the ground and twisting his jaunty fingers about the knuckle to recover my phone. As soon as it was mine again, I swiftly concealed it in my jeans and ran to my bag. Heated exhilaration fuelled that sprint to the rucksack, and when I looked up, I saw my companions were no more. Unaided and desperately surrounded, skates discarded on the floor and my belongings littered around me—I'd been here before.

My options were limited, but I was adamant not to lose a thing this time. Fear had vanished, and rational thought came in a vivid concoction of stubborn pride and determination. The injured man, the leader it seemed, began by undoing his belt buckle, easing out the leather strap and weighing up the steel fastener with his crippled hand. A malicious smile fastened across his cheeks. The first lash stung me hastily on protruding hip bone. Parchment-thin flesh tore, and in scanty retaliation, I went for a jab at the taller man. It missed. Whilst I was caught off balance, one of the smaller boys took a running leap to my kneecap, which brought me tumbling to the ground like a newborn lamb. But as fast as I was floored, I was up and took another swing at the man's face, and failed again. As I recollect, for reasons I can't fathom, I could hear nothing, and silently I endured blow after blow. Some were to my head and others to the belly; however, my futile defences never wore. All the while, they tired of beating me. I could sense it; the tussle dragged on, and the thieves fatigued. In a sudden moment of strength, I peered out of the foetal position I had cowered in, peeking through fingers and forearm to find my bearings. I glimpsed one of the younger lads wielding a matt-black canister. He sprayed it in my direction. I propped myself up, clueless, as the venomous liquid whipped diagonally across my face, and in an instant, my eyes and lips were ablaze. On my knees, I swung and jabbed aimlessly, intermittently wiping my eyes but to no avail, and the burning only worsened as more liquid trickled into my teary ducts, forcing my lids shut. Temporary blindness gave the younger ones an opportunity to scamper off with my belongings, and in a rare glimpse of clarity I saw my bag being snatched. Furious, I shouted and screamed, but not a note escaped from the muteness which entrapped me. The two men continued their tirade of whipping, never approaching too close to avoid catching an erratic blow. The assault drew to a close when their goading had become hoarse. I clamoured for a trade, a simple exchange of my bag for the phone. They had my house keys and bank cards, my journey and entry home. It sounds strange to me, even now, but from those intimate and violent moments we shared together, I knew that I could trust them. Sightlessly, I rummaged through my pockets and held it out at arm's length, anticipating its theft. Someone snatched it from my grip, and in return, my bag was thrown at me. The weight of it struck me flat on the belly, returning me reassuringly to the concrete.

The first sound that found me afterwards resembled the patter of footsteps, gently dissipating. I lay still for some time, curled up like a woodlouse around my rucksack, waiting for the sound to disappear. Every movement sent pain to the extremes of my body. Rolling on to my stomach, I gently worked myself back to crouching upon knees. I limped off into the open, to grey skies and the motorway above. Fires burnt strong in both eyes; it eased the soreness from bruises that pinched my muscles. A shoeless foot found itself inside a soft puddle; before it could saturate any further, I fell on to it on all fours, forehead and open eyes submerged as far its gritty depth allowed me, with eyebrows sweeping its mossy bed. I worked the shallow pool around my face and mouth, but the burning only worsened, and the softer features of my face blistered and cracked with the liquid as it crystallised. The searing wrought destruction on my eyes, blazing hotter than ever. Stepping out beside the motorway and into the spitting rain only added to its eroding effect. A pedestrian spotted me, and punctually I discovered myself in an ambulance.

Olive oil proved to be the simple solution for the burning, and the cause was police issue CS spray, which, unlike pepper spray, could not be washed out with water. I had agreed to give them a statement as soon as the burning subsided, and I waited there in hospital till the nurse came to wash off my face and the remaining ointment. I sat upright on the hydraulic bed and watched my legs swing freely below me, swirling in concentric circles. Thoughts of anger were the only ones that comforted, and my eyes began to water. I can still feel the coarse paper sheets that grazed my finger tips. I tried to distract myself from it, from that feeling of worthlessness—stripped of free will, beaten and robbed, then patched up, and left to repeat. I realised I was crying and couldn't remember a time before that I'd wept. It didn't help one bit, just self-indulgence; where was my pride then? I held my breath to slow the heart, till a more urgent need started me up again. Ripped finger holes blemished the sterile sheets I sat on, torn just slightly, and then fingers relaxed.

From the remnants of the crew that remained, we had all learnt to endure the cuts and bruises that skating threw at us. Falling unconscious and waiting in hospital wards had formed a part of our monthly routine. London had emerged more vengeful than the risk of skating itself, and the urge to carry protection strengthened as stories of others' misfortunes spread. Genu wielded his trusty 'Harry' the hammer in case, a tool of trade that was safe to carry, and a hideous armament in the wrong hands. I'd even seen him use it once, one time too many if he'd have asked me.

Anticipation—I detest the feeling; for good or for bad, it wrecks me with nerves. It's not the time itself that passes which forms the crux of the problem. With the event an inevitability, then neither can it be to blame. The real cause of my neurosis stems from that abhorrent tenseness which runs beneath the pores of my skin, bloating my body with acidic heat, directing my will with nothing but an impulse to skip and scurry in time. Isn't a feeling unproductive when it urges one to waste life's most precious commodity? I'm sure this immorality can be overridden with sense or, even simpler, with nonsense for that matter. If I am to discard any memory of the coming event or misplace knowledge of it by chance, wouldn't that put an end to it? Only then can I fully value the moments that pass me by. I want to forever feel the world around me and inhale with entire appreciation the environment I'm in, savouring everything at present, be it pleasurable or otherwise. The future is but a product of memories I haven't yet lost. So simply, all I aspire to do is forget what lies in front and try to retain all that passes me by. Though it is a struggle, since I'm prone to thinking too much and remembering very little, I hope that if I do get there, I'll be content. However, this conclusion I've reached by definition is counterproductive, since hope is just a form of anticipation, and now I'm over-thinking, again . . . and I'll stop, again, and continue with a lingering memory that I've remembered:

'He'll be here in an hour, so make sure you're ready and have all your stuff packed.'

'I'm not going! I wanna stay here.'

'Didecan, I'm sorry, but you know you have to go. It's just for the weekend!'

'Why do I have to go? I don't want to, I want to stay here with you! Why are you sending me to him?' She let out a heavy sigh and dried one eye *with her sleeve. Didecan softened his tone with her. 'Please, Mum, I really want to stay here, with you.' She turned away, averting her gaze to the window that overlooked the main road. He understood she had no choice in these matters; he'd testified in court and heard for himself that weekend visits were mandatory. He knew what he was obliged to do, but he never understood why. For those judges that ruled the proceedings had no idea of how he felt or any idea of how it affected Sister. Sure she was strong enough to endure it all, but that didn't make it all right. Didecan joined her side and peered out of the window too, and they waited together quietly for a while.*

He would always park on the opposite side of the road, making sure he was only just in sight if they happened to be looking out. He'd telephone the house from his mobile to prompt them of his arrival and never knocked or crossed to their side of the road, couldn't risk an encounter with her. Then he'd hang up before anyone could answer and sit waiting for two little silhouettes to disappear from the window. Sister normally hugged her boy at the door and let him cross the road on his own, but not this time. Didecan tried his luck, determined not to budge. He sat barricaded with his back flat against the door. Calm as ever, Sister whisked his delicate body up over her shoulder, unlocked the door with her free arm, and continued down the stairs to the road. He screamed, and kicked, and cried, yelping half-breathed pleas not to see Mr P between fits of tears. She marched coldly across the road; Didecan folded feet first over one shoulder. Mr P's car was parked close by, and he stood beside it stationary, listening attentively to the pleas that spilt from the mouth of his only remaining child. 'I don't want to see him, I'm not seeing him, please, Mum, pleeease.' She handed him to Mr P. Passed from shoulder to shoulder, tears dampened the forearms of both parents, Didecan never got to see Sister leave; his fury had got the better of him and now he was in the single place he dreaded most.

He waited, affronted, in the passenger seat, waited for Mr P to sit beside him and start the car, waited for the day to be over, and then for the next after that. Their journey to Essex was always in bitter silence. His attention adhered to the passing scenery that flew past in ebbs of blurry clarity. Bushy greens of leafy suburbia would predictably turn to blocks of grey on entering streams of motorway. An hour's journey would go by. Spent head pressed up against the passenger window, padding gentle shocks to his brow, absorbing the slow inhale of that humid stench which came from Mr P. In a short time, he saw nothing through those wide-awake eyes of his and remembered nothing of the weekend that was to follow.

FRAGMENT 11

After all the troubles he faced dwelling on turgid streets, a little nervous tension struck him at the prospect of starting university. It would be was his chance to introduce himself to the social norms that most others of his age took part in, things like meeting in bars and partying till late, all that he neglected in youth. Money had never been an issue before his self-imposed theft restrictions, but it had prevented him from indulging in those pleasures and quickly he came to realise its worth. He started working full time at the sandwich shop opposite his university. A minimal income made him watch his pennies closely, and a thrifty conscience made sure his only spending went on items that couldn't be easily pinched. So he feasted on hot dinners, takeaway meals, and pints of beer at the pub, knowing it couldn't be had any other way.

In the flat, Didecan was the oddest and only male present, renting from two prosperous graphic designers who shared the flat, the smallest room was his. He had just enough space for a single bed, plus storage beneath it. So cosy was his room that the door could open just a fraction, before rebounding off the edge of his sleeping mattress, but it suited his measly stature adequately. He often thought that the two women living with him must have known what type of individual they would attract, to reside in such a small mess, so he kept to himself, and as usual spent most of his day out of the house.

Engineering turned out to be the only course at his university as regimented as school. He expected more girls, and had never seen so many Chinese people all at once. Students were the scholarly types and passionate about their field of work, obsessed even. He learnt that was to be expected when choosing such high academia. Lectures stretched longer than ever, up to three hours even, and paired with the fatigue he suffered from working full time at the sandwich shop, it left his concentration in tatters. Over time, he found it more productive to simply copy notes from the whiteboard in a haze of classic rock n roll which reeled from his walkman than try and focus in class.

In the first week, each academite received a reading list from their department. For Engineering, twelve necessary books were needed in order to follow the course, and each book cost up to a hundred pounds. There were few students with jobs outside of classes, and Didecan was one of a minority of less-fortunate individuals who needed to work in order to pay his living costs. The books seemed an impossible task, and he never envisaged falling back on his previous methods; he never wanted to, but to fit into such financially demanding circles, it seemed a necessary malpractice. Before the week was up, he had swiftly thieved all the reading materials he would require for the coming years at university, and he vowed that would be the last time he would resort to old methods. It was no secret to his classmates how he had come to possess the workbooks, and he saw no shame in it, for in those that sat alongside him, he saw a generation fated to a path society had spared for them. He admired those individuals who had their lives all planned out, those who thought little of the now and more of what lay ahead, but never quite had the courage or sanity to join them.

The first term of university had fascinated him, and again he observed the simple tribes which formed from lost children trying to find their clique in life, like the fanatical Muslims who forever craved a good debate and the rosy-cheeked rugby boys who spent more time in the pub than in lectures. He loathed socialising with the rest of his classmates, and clubbing in particular; he just couldn't comprehend the appeal. Queuing almost an hour to pay at the door, to possibly be let inside a room filled with the very same people whom he waited outside for free with. It was too loud for him to talk and too costly to drink. He wondered why they all went, when the rest looked to be having a worse time than him. His Engineering department were easy to spot at any nightclub, pressed rigid up against the walls, one hand clasping a tepid drink and the other delving down a trouser pocket. At best, Didecan was left peeved when most night outs were spent in vain attempting to enter bars and clubs with age, clothing, and gender requirements. Spending entire wet nights waiting for another expectedly disappointing end to a day, and for no good reason he could fathom, he had sensed his peers only went to meet expectations of getting drunk and partying, rather than for their own enjoyment. In defiance, he ceased to follow the social trends that his establishment had to offer and came to the realisation that nobody in his year group was quite comfortable with what they were doing, himself included, yet they continued to do so.

He took natural refuge from that precarious world in his work. It was a strange feeling to be so at ease in that environment, especially being the only native English speaker working there. From the very beginning, nobody knew quite where to place him. The Eastern Europeans assumed he was Bangladeshi, and the Bangladeshis regarded him an Englishman; in reality, he had never felt so English in his life now that he was surrounded entirely by other nationalities. Marty's Sandwich Shop rests in the geographical centre of London. It was a claustrophobic eatery which stayed open late enough to pick up the drunken clubbing crowd from their waltz home in the morning, making it the busiest sandwich shop for miles. Shifts comprised of ten-hour stints, four days a week. Didecan would clock in after finishing lectures, and leave at three in the morning, giving him a healthy five hours of sleep before having to wake up for classes the same morning, smelling of freshly prepped dough. And on the leftover days, he skated, with not a day going by that he returned home before midnight. In this business, he rid himself of the indulgence of sleep, living every day long and full.

He worked untiringly at Marty's as he knew no other way; the excruciatingly tedious working hours and busy periods allowed him to switch off from the stresses of university. But even then, he couldn't comprehend how the other full-time workers dealt with the repetition of work on a daily basis, where often one's hands weren't coordinated enough to keep up with the demand without bumping into one another. By far the most ardent employee at Marty's was Cador. A young Slovakian new to London and its ways, he was an extraordinary character with exceptional humour and work ethic, endowed with a natural sociability that far outweighed his grasp of the English language. His speech came quickly, in rapid bursts ridden with grammatical injustices, though wit rang through in every sentence. Forever the entertainer and centre of attention, he proved to be a constant source of amusement, but Didecan sensed in him something that didn't add up. He only had a handful of friends in the shop. Didecan believed with certainty that it was a result of his overt hostility towards other immigrants. He would orate to Didecan on how the Bangladeshis lacked social skills, and had alienated himself from the Poles and Hungarians, whom he openly admitted to not trusting for historical purposes. After he discovered that Didecan was no Bangladeshi and unlike any Englishmen he had met, they had got along quite well.

The governing men who managed the shop rarely made themselves present or carried much presence when present, which meant rules and regulations at Marty's were near non-existent. For two young working boys it was ideal, with unlimited food that could be used for vital bargaining. Cador's usual tactic was to question girls on their thoughts of Barry White. If they were a fan, they were awarded a free sandwich, no strings attached, and if they weren't, they paid. But they wouldn't know that. His well-formulated theory behind the inquest relied on their return to the shop; it eliminated messy first conversations, and considering they had already shared an altogether more profound encounter, it allowed them to talk without restraint the second time round. His style of ruthless extroversion, along with a rigorous ethos to accomplish, allowed his English to improve weekly, for Didecan's and to his own benefit. His talents, however, were not without vice, for Didecan found it impossible to draw the line between Cador's intoxication and his impulsiveness. Alcohol was so deeply ingrained in his blood that it could not be easily separated from his personality. He incorporated it into his working life, slipping vodka by his drinking cup and encouraging others to do the same. Didecan had sectioned Cador as a heedless genius with a Machiavellian's ability to win favour through contumacious egoism; he'd even confided to Didecan that the only things that mattered to him were development in language and his finances, not forgetting, of course, the sustenance of his humour.

They formed the backbone of that busy little sandwich shop, working at the busiest hours of the night. The lax environment allowed them to consider the shop as their own, to do as they wished, meeting and conversing with more people in one night than any university socialite could achieve in a week. The interactions they created between colleagues and clientele seemed limitless, feeding an endless supply of demanding customers at all hours of the day; though soon, their boisterous fun and games were to come to a halt with the arrival of a new Pole to the shop.

Of all the detestable nationalities Cador harboured a hatred for, it was the Polish who took the blame for most of the world's disquietude. From the way they enunciated in English to the clothes they wore, his repulsion found no end. Didecan thought his friend's prejudice was a response to the sudden filling of the city with Polish migrants, who were seen and heard everywhere, but nobody else seemed to care. It didn't help that the last three new recruits at Marty's were all Poles, and the arrival of one more only strengthened his suspicions of the Polish owner hiring with an agenda.

However, May was different. She was an abnormally private old girl who didn't cosy in with the other staff or attempt to take part in any unnecessary conversation. Overall, her features were dark, and her skin was so contrastingly pallid that it looked wet, almost as if the sheer blackness of her hair and pupils were so infinitely inky that they stripped the colour clean from the rest of her body. That precise difference, he could hear it in her voice. She had impeccable English, though a heavy accent; Cador would often arrive to work with a greeting of 'Mornink' and was fast to ridicule. Her natural scent was that of cigarette with which she shared an eternal and uncompromising attachment, though small habits in her craving made Didecan think of it as something more than a simple nicotine addiction. He watched her pull at the final joyous drag of it; hesitantly she would take a last regretted look at the object that induced her to such ecstasy, docile eyes of pure satisfaction; then between thumb and forefinger, she would flick the ungodly butt as far as her slight fingers could muster, spreading a guttural fold of resentment across her forehead whilst doing so. The two friends watching her ritual came to think it was all she ever lived for. Her reclusiveness had intrigued Didecan, and slowly he began to strip apart her enigma in the depths of the prep basement downstairs, where they readied frozen meats for the following day. It had proved impossible for him to get any conversation out of her upstairs in the light of day; she froze at the prospect of serving strangers or speaking to somebody she wasn't comfortable with, and whispered but single cordial words when in the company of work colleagues. Though she spoke to Didecan and actively sought him in the basement to think out loud. And they talked of things Didecan had never thought to contemplate before: of love and purpose, their existence, music and mood, and death. Their conversations in the basement were always heavy, conclusions stewed, thickening the air, making it unbreathable for those who happened to wander past. Her view on the world was rigid, set around a morbid logic, and it was the reason Didecan adored her so much. After hearing his own thoughts aloud, he believed they agreed on very similar principles, but his were by no means as radical as May's—a simple matter of age, he believed. They both held established views on the non-existence of an afterlife and on the futility of faith; on many occasions, they concurred that intelligence was a burden to happiness, yet there were aspects of their conversations that troubled him, that left him uneasy. After talking to her, he thought of nothing else. Her ideas spiralled in circles around him yet never seemed to do him any good, seeds that never settled, and rendered him restless and weary.

He found himself spending more time with May, and in turn, he discovered a little deeper into himself and the world around him, never fully realising why she felt so much at ease with him. He had never cared to share his thoughts with anyone else, fearing they wouldn't understand, but May was somebody who could not only comprehend things but help evaluate his understanding of matters. And throughout their underground exchanges, their friendship remained a wholly platonic affair, which made it all the more pure, but he made sure to keep his distance at times he couldn't fully grasp her madness.

FRAGMENT 12

'Ham prep' was Didecan's most loathsome task at Marty's. It involved laboriously peeling layers of semi-defrosted pork slices apart for hours, which was near impossible when every pork chunk came centrally fused by frost. She arrived to work in high spirits, and the very sight of her that instant appeared strange to him, uplifting, gleaming even. He naturally thought she had changed her look; maybe she had dyed her hair, or was wearing different makeup, or drunk. 'Didecan, I'm goink to have a baby!'

'What . . . How?' he questioned her, trying his utmost not to smile. 'I didn't have my period, and started getting cramps. And felt sick all week. Like trowin up, look!' She rolled up her shirt a little from the waist to reveal a small pot belly, which had evidently swollen.

'With who? Have you taken a test?'

'I don't know. I'm goin' to buy one after work, but I'm so sure. I've always wanted to have a baby. You know, something that is worth to stay livink for, to teach him everythink you know. I don't want a girl. I don't know what I would do if it's a girl, they're too emotional. I couldn't do that.'

'When was the last time you had sex?'

'I didn't since my last boyfriend, maybe seven months ago.'

'Then how is it possible?'

'I don't know, but look!' The sight of her ripe belly convinced them both. It made no sense to him, but the signs were there. He had never seen her so happy; it was what she had always wanted she told him—normality, he supposed, a baby, and soon a family, some sense of fitting in. She swore Didecan to secrecy and mentioned the matter no further. He wondered if she might have shied from telling him the truth, that maybe she was seeing someone and keeping it a secret from him, but couldn't think of why she would do it.

The following day, he provoked her for the test results, but she remained silent, evading him time and again, busying herself in subdued work for most of the shift. Her response came to him at the end of the day, when the time was right. And without a word, she revealed a strip of shiny white plastic with a single thin red line split across its display, and a trickling tear fell effortlessly down the left side of her pale cheek. She ignored it. 'It means I'm not pregnant . . . I know I'm crazy, but not like this.' He endeavoured to comfort her, and she shot him a look of such vulnerable intimacy that he lost his train of thought. 'It's called a phantom pregnancy. It's when you want it so bad that your mind cheats your body into thinkin and feelink pregnant,' she explained. 'But you never mentioned wanting a baby before.'

'I always wanted one. I know it sounds stupid, but I miss him so much right now. I felt so close to him when he was in me, and now I've lost him.'

'I get it.' He didn't know what to say or even if he should say something. Her eyes were bloodshot and mascara bled down into the deepest grooves of her lips. 'But nothing's really changed,' he added unsurely. She collapsed gently on to his chest. Didecan embraced her for a moment, giving her time to settle her emotions, drying her eyes in his work shirt. It was the closest they had physically been, and Didecan was fully aware of it. As much as he cared for her, he was frightened of getting too close; it was her madness, or intellect, depending on which way he looked at it. The following morning, she appeared at work as usual, belly flat and eyes deep as wells.

FRAGMENT 13

May completed her masters in Chemistry at one of Krakow's most revered universities of science. Flourishing academically, she had become the highest achieving student in her class, which delivered her promptly to a laboratory job in her chosen field. Beside her childhood boyfriend, she led a devoted life on the outskirts of that youthful city, but their picturesque path together was short-lived. At twenty-five, their relationship stumbled to a close. Lost and distraught, she left her job and fled to a small village in Alaska, seeking respite. The urge to settle down and form a family charred her inside, but it's reality seemed no more than a fascination; too late in life to start again, she deemed herself an outcast to happiness. So she set a deadline to her misery, a measure at which she sought to cease her existence, at the seasoned age of thirty. And felt that if she had not managed to amend her place in the world by then, there would be no point in continuing any further.

Didecan understood her use of the deadline implicitly. It put a tangible value on life and meant that every passing year had a purpose; it made living more productive, living for the present, knowing it would not return again, and made death predictable. He shared no desire to settle down or nurture a family, but craved something far simpler. Contentedness was what he willed, and the feeling of fulfilment that comes with it—very different from happiness, which shines and fades with the weather, but peace in having security of mind. It took some deliberation, but he felt it wasn't too much to ask, a perfectly reasonable aspiration he thought, and gave himself plenty of time, plotting his expiry at thirty-three years of living.

He and May grew together, exploring the intricacies of each other's thoughts. Even Cador began to take up a keen interest in her, who debated whether she was alike any Pole or any girl even that he had known before. Both of them were ridden with quirks and idealisms; Didecan could see the natural attraction. Every morning, after closing, they would continue to drink at one of their houses, and alcohol served as their platform to speak with absolute freedom, no matter how morbid or offensive it may be. May saw no further into it than a mere sharing of philosophies, though Cador craved a little more. The times they spent together were caught eternally in debate, dissecting and tearing apart each other's take on life, the sort of arguments that had no definite end besides who deemed themselves triumphant. And in time, like Didecan, he became all too conscious of her destructive innocence.

Egoism had driven Cador to the borders of sanity in attempts to save her from herself. Still he defended his feelings bluntly, likening her to the sandwich special for the week ahead. 'Teriyaki', he explained to Didecan, and in order to sell it for the week ahead, it needed to be stocked and prepared. He claimed to run his emotions like a business. Didecan could see the funny side of it but believed truly that his friend had journeyed too far with May to brush her off as a sandwich.

The three of them were inseparable, sharing a bleak and analytic perspective on their surroundings. They cut out the pretence and small talk that riddled their society—that of faith, hope, and inanity. Very soon, May and Cador moved in together, sharing a small studio flat that was cheap and convenient within walking distance of Marty's. It became a rendezvous for the trio to air their opinions on life and compare their tastes over numerous bottles of vodka till the sun beamed the next morning. Their room overlooked the high street, perched over a questionable sauna with tinted windows and bead-curtained doors. The dark and smoke-filled setting matched May's demeanour and malnourished form, and on each journey Didecan made to their vampiric dwelling, he witnessed Cador visibly paler and ill at ease. The intensity of her melancholia had lured him, breathing abstract thought fresh through both their minds, without consideration or restraint. Cador's stray feelings for May became an obsession, and as he drew closer to her, his lust for something deeper grew. May's darkness had enveloped him, and only alcohol remained to refuel their energies night after night. Didecan rarely saw them sober outside of work. The reality they had sculpted for themselves within their tiny abode didn't allow sobriety, and at the bottom of a bottle there was the numbness that they yearned all day, and quenched the minute they ended work.

Her most bitter battle was fought within herself; the constant effect of considering life easier if she only thought less consumed her. Her reasoning foresaw two paths. She could live a credulous existence that was simple and happy, or she could choose to think as clearly as she did and stay trapped in fits of sorrow. She craved the former and sought it through vodka to smoothen those thoughts that assailed her.

In numbness, they felt the sole presence of each other, encased in a mist of music which shrouded them, making sleep fast and heavy, and thought, little and deep. Cador's joviality at work had disappeared, and he shared his humour with no one. Building a cloak around himself so impenetrable, he resisted even May and Didecan; they could do nothing to induce a smile or a response from him in that state of abstinence, but they both knew how to end it. Be it a shot of vodka or a sip of beer it mattered little, a small intake of toxicant was all he needed to graciously bloom into his previous shade of charm and wit. Didecan would take every opportunity to accompany the pair in their inebriated state, and he drank to their levels just to catch a glimpse of his late friend. Whilst the cover of shade thickened towards midnight and the atmosphere grew dense with cigarette smoke, AC/DC roared out of tiny portable speakers and vodka bottles gathered in the spaces between drinkers. Cador appeared through the thickest of it, an immolated apparition shining through a fog of gloom, just momentarily, prior to passing out for the night. Their friendship together was soon hindered by Cador's increasing protectiveness over May. The thought of her and Didecan getting too intimate entwined itself in his jealousy, and in turn, his manner towards Didecan deteriorated. They joked little and saw less of what they admired in one another. When Didecan eventually left his job at the sandwich shop, he saw Cador only whilst visiting May, often sulking in the backdrop, silent and disruptive, and he realised it was too late.

A party was held at the flat. Friends from work joined the trio in celebration, for nothing at all in particular. It stemmed from an idea they discussed, a spontaneous appreciation of the moment, as preposterous and meaningful as the more typical celebrations such as birthdays and anniversaries. And each guest invited brought with them a bottle and high spirits for the occasion. May and Didecan sat apart from the group, perched on the edge of the window sill that overlooked the canopy of the sauna below. They talked as they always did, of nothing and everything; it was how they enjoyed their time together, and Cador sat closely behind, tossing an occasional gruff look at them to make his discomfort felt. The two continued on unaffected, engrossed in conversation till Cador's frustrations got the better of him. He retired outside on to the pavement beneath them and began working his way through a fresh pack of Lucky Strikes. Didecan had drunk two full cans of beer dry in the time it took her to draw her last ceremonious drag of cigarette. Flicking it out into the street below, it skipped a little on the tarmac before the fragile embers burnt themselves out. Endless conversations with her gave Didecan some insight into predicting her mood, undoubtedly the more spirit she consumed in eager conversation, the more her own would harden. Talk would indisputably shift to her suppositions of 'life as a curse' and her defencelessness in the matter. He had near developed a sixth sense in forecasting when her depression would erupt and eventually fade; it came in cycles, and he could tell that this was the start of a difficult few days for her. 'Have you ever thought of just slipping away, Didecan?' She only ever addressed him so prominently by name when it came to matters she felt were of the utmost importance. She had an odd way of pronouncing it, or mispronouncing it even, something that unnerved him and something he couldn't quite put his finger on.

'Like what? Ending it?'

'Yeah, you know, it's the hardest thin' you can do, your mind is program for survivink . . .'

'I think if you want to . . . do it. You just do it. I don't see the point in dwelling on it, when you've had enough that's it, no? That's what I'd do.'

'I could do it now,' she sighed. There was a momentary pause before she slid. Her hips drifted gracefully off the narrow seam of the window sill, and her slender body followed, ripping the canopy of the sauna below. She floated noiselessly through the clear night air, hitting the pavement bare feet first, emitting a soft woollen thud as she set down. She shrieked cries that guaranteed how awkwardly she had fallen; he leapt out after her and landed solidly at her side. Her crippled feet turned blue under the orange glow of the electric street light; then a shadow fell on them both. Cador stood over them, face flushed white with fury; he looked on at Didecan without a word.

A faint glow from the following day warmed the pavement on which they stood barefoot and intoxicated. Didecan's first attempts to prop her up to her feet ended in more tears, so he picked her fractured body up whole in his arms and carried her up the narrow staircase that led up to the flat. Her drunken head bobbed lifelessly at every creaking movement. He left her in the bathroom, away from the bustle of the party. Cador vehemently followed, watching in the doorway. They both spoke very briefly, in words that expelled as javelins, and Didecan departed, as requested. Cador's demand to sever links with him and May forever had been granted. He waited a few minutes to be certain Didecan was out of sight before he escorted May to hospital, where they identified hairline fractures honeycombed throughout her left heel and ankle. They set her in cast and advised her not to walk for at least three months.

Several weeks of depression passed, with May housebound and only her thoughts to keep her company. Cador worked double time at Marty's to keep up with their rent payments, but whether he was home or not, the feeling of claustrophobia consumed her, knowing that it was neither him nor those four walls that maddened her.

My consciousness is stirred by rigid turns, and finally I wake up with eardrums filled by the monotonous vibrations that old and rusted motor car's emanate. The movements of my disgruntled stomach follow suit.

Lungs are heavy, and warm re-breathed air makes all my body want to drift back away to a solemn sleep. A crack in my sight fills me with pipettes of luminance, familiar shades flicker by, and I recognise my surroundings. Blue rails, corroded red brick, passing the police station and the house I once lived as a boy, West Hampstead. Warm feelings of home and youth coat me in comfort; it impels to send me off to a slumber. I turn to see my mother; she's driving, though she sleeps heavy. And the car continues on with pace; endless red-and-blue glossed doors and hedgerows stream by in flashes of green and multicolour.

How much longer can her slumber last? How would it feel to be inside a plane crash in a free fall? Giving myself up to the inevitable, would I panic or would I sit and appreciate? Both outcomes fruitless. Subdued, I lie placid, so I contemplate. This is different. I can stop this. I just need to wake her up. It's simple, and it's not the same. How long have I been thinking of that destiny, and why do I still think? My thoughts are careful, deliberated, and teasingly, the car still moves on. But wait! Why so? For so many times I've wanted to, and now? A change of heart? No. It makes no difference either way. It's the moment I've been living for, a convenient opportunity for me to slip out. The road veers away at her side, and I edge smoothly towards that blur of colours, hastily more vivid. I panic and scream in a heart's thud.

Incoherent yelling fills the coach they are sleeping in peacefully. It's 4 a.m. on the way to Teman Negara. She looks at him, frightened and angry. 'What are you doing!?'

'I . . . a dream, 'm sorry,' he gasped.

The coach participants turn away one head by one; he should feel embarrassed by what just almost happened to him. It was only a dream, but the decision was real, a conscious choice. He believes it, and lies assured that it would have been the same outside of dream. His moist hand intertwines with hers, and he sits back half awake, frightened to drift.

FRAGMENT 14

I saw the young lads wearing my old school uniform on the tube; these boys, they're made to dress like penguins, all trussed up in black and white, chests held high with pert pink lips. Their gait differs from the natural saunter of boys worldwide. It's more upright and stiff, like the waddle of a pendulum, mirrored rigidly by their ties. All they needed to complete the look was orange shoes, if they were allowed it. Penguins, I say to the lot of them! They're proud and young and privileged, and they know it. But what can one do about it? Youth, it's the same excuse I've been using for years. That which allows them to follow and flaunt simultaneously, and the same one that permits me to stray—it won't last too long, but it's still here in the now. The final year of my degree's round the corner, I should probably start to look for a proper job like the rest of the engineering lot, or at least something to pay off the bills for the next few months. Not saying quitting Marty's was a bad call, I reckon if I'd have stayed on much longer, I would have flunked this year. Luckily, I ain't doing too badly now sitting on average grades, even if my sleeping patterns are all over the place. Uni's ending in a month for summer holidays, so I guess now's as good a time as any to start printing CVs off en masse. I do repudiate the whole formality surrounding them. It's just so impersonal and, needless to say, insecure. Not only are most CVs rife in fallacy but they're ultimately unmemorable. Was there a time we ever found work simply? Brief chats or on the spot interviews? It'd cut out all this messy CV business, especially in hospitality where it's all about personality and flair. OK, so it's not the most functional approach, I do understand, so I'll have to compromise, maybe I'll just bring the one in my pocket as a last resort. First stop, I think, should be that little chicken restaurant around the corner. Can't stand the idea of looking into an internship, or following a career in engineering. That'd be the easy option. At least the people at the chicken shop look like they're having fun; they're always pissing about, not to mention there's a pretty cute supervisor working there, not stereotypically stunning, but sort of quirky looking.

Couldn't have picked a worst day for all this. Should have at least tried before skating, when my hands weren't yet blackened by city grime and when my trousers were free from gritty streaks. I'm here now anyway, and it looks quiet; besides, if I look trampy, it's just a conversation; if I can't get a job here, then how the hell do I hope to get a job anywhere else? The front windows here are always pristine, yet I've never see anybody washing them, midnight cleaners maybe . . . ah and she's working. I can't really go on in looking like this, can I? That body is perfection! Petite in all the right spots with just the slightest of curve around the hips, have to stop looking. She's got to be Eastern European; I'm going with Polish by the looks of it, her hair especially; blonde, messy, shoulder length. It looks unwashed and even a little greasy. I imagine it smells amazing. What's the worst that can happen? I definitely can't stand staring through this window all day.

I was right. She smells better than I could ever have dreamt. She's a smoker, though. Has to be with a voice like that, not husky, just a little dry, sandpaperish. It's imperfection that makes her so perfect. We've talked for so long, I almost forgot why I've come. We haven't even started work talk yet. She must be a little bored. I would be if it's as quiet as this all the time. I don't think I've ever come across someone with so much genuine enthusiasm, or maybe she's into me too? I'd love to be able to speak like she does, open and confident all the time; it's more the consistency I struggle with. And there's a certain something in her tone, something vulnerable; it's not apparent but it's there. She's smiling at me. I should say something. It's not a pretty smile, but it shows tenderness, fragility even. Why don't I say something? Her skin's slightly chapped around it, and two tiny dimples tunnel into the corners of her lips. I feel so light-headed, so timid. I can't look at it any more. If I could go red, I'm sure I would. I can feel my cheeks blushing. I suppose having this much melanin does have the odd benefit. I've lost it. Talk. Talk something, talk work, where do I start? What are the hours like? Pay? Anything. But we've already spoken about it, I'm sure. I remember now it wasn't even ten minutes ago. There is a position available, she told me. Give it a week, she said. Shit, she must think I'm simple if I keep asking her the same questions, or worse that I'm not even listening to her. I should go. A handshake?

It's a lot colder out than it was before. That was bloody awkward. I can't believe I screwed up at the last hurdle. I've always been crap at farewells. In hindsight, I should have left her with a couple of continental kisses on the cheek; it's too late now, but it would have been better than an eager handshake. I suppose the chat went pretty well.

Two weeks had gone by in a blink. Coursework hung over me so eminently, I failed to realise that my phone call never came. Looking back, I'm sure the job was as good as mine, and now it feels so unattainable, now that I want it more than ever. She must have used me, I don't know what for, but maybe it was her polite way of letting people down. I even remembered her name. Perhaps she's equally as manipulative as I am? As verbose and as easy to get along with, and she was that friendly with everyone; why do I always think of myself as the special case? Fuck you, ego, who plays tricks on my sense of perspective, and I'm sure more times than I'm fully conscious of. No real loss. There are lots of other places to find work in this city. Well, I definitely can't eat there any more, especially if she's working; that's the worst of it.

———

FRAGMENT 15

Why do I bother calling Py out to skate? It's excruciating. He's always trying to lecture you on something or the other. It's worse when you're left alone with him, like now; Freemason conspiracies, and his proof all on a dollar note that he holds to him like a safety blanket; all the evidence is on there, apparently. Where does this 'need to spread the word' mentality come from? It's probably just easier if I don't argue back, but I bloody hate doing that. I'll just walk and grunt at him once in a while. At least when we're skating, we don't have to talk to each other. It's just the walking in between parts.

That can't be her, can it? At times like these, I wish my memory would serve me better. It looks like her. I'm picturing her in her uniform and there are similarities, but the lady across the road, she's more elegant, softer than Juliette, a little more sophisticated, or maybe just older. It could be her. She walks so quickly, no doubt an effect of working in restaurants for so long, and this woman across the road looks so rushed. She only looks forward, at where her next step will fall, not like me who takes it all in. I know these paving stones so well, every crack and crevice, I need not look down. These streets are my own and everyone else's too. It's what is inside these buildings that remains an illusion to me. At the top, and in through their windowpanes, I'll peer through to their ceilings. Probably an office or computer-drenched room of sorts. I look into secret chambers where grown children dedicate their lives and time, each chamber with a purpose, and behind each purpose an individual. So I look up and question, not ahead or below, for what's ahead and underneath me on the pavement is something we all share, so why grow bored? Up there is how I'll find my way. I'll cherish every moment, and for just one moment, I'll cherish her. 'Didecan! Hey, Didecan!' Ah, shit! She's seen me, probably thinks I was staring at her like some pervert, and she's crossing over. 'Hey, Juliette! You remember my name?'

'How could I forget? Ah, you're skating again! That's cool. It must be how you keep so fit, eh?' Is that flirting? Or just childishness? It's pretty funny, whichever one it was. 'I suppose, yeah, I'd call it skinny.' A weak attempt at diffidence, well done, Didecan. 'Stop being modest, eh. I'm sorry we never got back to you about the job. It's been so busy at the moment, but you're at the top of our pile of things to do . . . Actually, why don't you come in tomorrow morning for a trial? Can you?' I've got a lecture tomorrow, but I could always pick up the notes from a mate afterwards, it wouldn't make much difference, considering I never pay attention anyway. 'Perfect, so black shoes and black trousers and I'll see you at ten. Maybe you should shave too. My boss will be there, and you'll want to make a good impression, innit?' That was a sarcastic *'innit'*, she's definitely got a weird way of speaking, or maybe she's mocking my English accent. I don't sound cockney. Working with her's going to be a lot of fun I can tell. Two charismatic pecks on the cheek this time, and we'll part ways. Why do I have to plan out everything?

The business runs by the firm and fair hand of Pangloss, whom I have the pleasure of sitting with for a final interview. He asks a lot of questions, short questions, ones that beckon long replies, and most of which I don't have the answer to and probably never will do. Who in the world really knows what they want to do in life, how do you answer that truthfully? And considering I've only just met you, how do I know what I hope to achieve from working for you or your establishment. Perhaps I'll acquire a gaze as insightful as yours, or maybe when my hair thins to that extent, I'll take a page out of your book, cut my losses, and shave the whole lot. Is that what you want to hear? So honesty is what you want; if not, it's certainly what you'll have. So am I naive in telling you that I have no idea? Judging by the look you've just thrown back at me, apparently so. I suppose you think me a liar and wonder why I'm studying engineering if I don't know what I want to do. Well, I ask myself the same thing. Maybe I should have come prepared or made something up, anything apart from the truth, and now he thinks I'm bullshitting to pass the interview. And why does he keep staring at me so intently? I'll shake his hand and leave. A firm professional handshake'll seal the deal.

He's asked me to sit and wait. We've shaken hands but haven't yet said goodbye; does that mean we don't shake again when we finally go our separate ways? How do I always find a way to make the last impression the most memorably awkward?

This Pangloss character seems an almost mythical creature, middle-aged and Irish, telling me rather bluntly that he's had affiliations with the IRA prior to falling into the grips of alcoholism. Is he trying to frighten me or playing a fatherly 'been there, done that' role? I'm assuming it's a form of indoctrination, in the salvation that is 'the business'. It's brought him out of the darkness and it can 'save you too' type of thing! It would explain those quivering old baby blue eyes, soft and drilling; they intensify in deep thought. Surely it's a juxtaposition of demeanour being so warm and edgily intense, clearly a madman. He's hung on to every syllable I've blurted, depositing it into his memory banks for later processing, I'm sure. I guess he thinks he's met loads of people like me in his time and I'm just another hapless student. In all honesty, I haven't said much to prove him wrong.

Back so soon? Probably haven't given you much to think about. And there's that stare again. You're loving this; I bet you enjoy this part the most, the 'sorry you're not up to scratch' part of the job. I don't suppose it'd be much fun working for a sadist anyway. Maybe it's for the best. But I'm hired, you say. You're giving me a chance? I don't understand, why? But thanks, more importantly thanks to Juliette. I'm sure she's had a part to play in this, can't believe she wants me here.

The work's not too hard, nothing like Marty's. It's better managed too. So many rules and restrictions make better business and, oddly enough, keep the staff sweet, knowing their place and position. The trickiest thing for me now is getting my head around the stark contrast of life outside of this servile work. I'm fine cleaning up under people's feet and around fetid toilet bowls. I'm not the squeamish type, but the abuse we took from hungry customers on a daily basis was savage. Nobody would think to address a stranger on the street like they would to staff at the chicken shop, because we can't talk back, and I've lost count of the times I've fought the urge to walk out because of power-tripping clientele. Compare that to the few days a week I get to skate. We're shooting for a local skate flick now, so always have a cameraman handy. Every session's carefully planned with a list of spots, tricks, and angles for the day to encompass a variety of different backgrounds and obstacles for the shoot. There were times we entertained crowds of passers-by for hours whilst capturing a trick. Times we had entire council estates in an uproar, families cheering behind window panes at soaring heights. I'd tear myself away from this to clean ketchup stains off the floor and be sworn at by chicken enthusiasts waiting fifteen minutes for food. No wonder they've hired a nutcase to run the shop; nobody else could do it. Though, he does run a tight ship and certainly knows how to get the most out of the team. I've never seen anything like it before. He treats us all like a family, or how I imagine he would treat his family. The Irish are a nation of large families, so maybe that's why. I'm the new guy here and haven't needed to try whatsoever. They've welcomed me into every conversation I'd wander past, and to each after work party. It's unbelievable to think there's not one outsider in this restaurant, a laudable quality, is it not? Everyone's from distant and different parts of the world, which, I reckon, helps the whole team dynamic—cuts out the natural herding instinct you find when similar nationalities and mother tongues group together. We get along real well, partying as hard as we work, and it's all Pangloss' doing. He cares so much about us, it's unhealthy. It won't last long. I give it a few years before he quits or gives himself a heart attack. He suffers fits of anger, and they're getting worse. They say you're always hurt most by the ones you love; well, that's just it.

Juliette's totally wasted here. She's got this dynamic with people, and I don't know where she's picked it up. I do think about it a lot. I can't mimic her. Frankly, it wouldn't suit me; people would begin to ask questions. But I try to find patterns. Is it what she says, or how she says? Or just that it's she who says it? She's met tons of people over the years, and I've noticed she's got the knack of knowing precisely what people want, or rather making people think they know what they want. I've got a lot to learn from her. She's wasted here and, in all honesty, so is everybody else. Pedro's a practising lawyer in Brazil, and Burmese Brenda's a nurse back home; they work constantly. Twelve-hour shifts at minimum wage, and for what? To improve their English? What stirs me the most is that they never complain. It'll only be the imbecilic that talk down to them and they just take it, all whilst toiling at extraction canopies and grills without an ill word. It took me some time, but I understand it now. It's simply because they can, and if it's physically achievable, then why should one shy away? The older lot have a confident comprehension of the world, and it makes me consider that no one is ever above, that we all just exist. These principles have never been verbalised, but it's more than apparent in the way we all work. I'll want to adopt this approach.

FRAGMENT 16

So she tells me she's bisexual but doesn't like to be put in boxes; what a tale if not for telling me sooner, and she decides to wait until now to tell me she's got a girlfriend. She never lied to me, and yeah, I was the only one not to know. I'm indifferent; we're still the same people. Things are just more challenging now. And I want her more than anything. I'll correct myself, I don't want her, I want 'that', and I see 'that' in her, that unattainable friend and partner, so close. We walk home together after work; sure, it's tacky, but I look forward to those walks. My entire day exists for nothing else but being beside her, in parks or sitting on pavements—it matters not, as long as she's nearby. I know that smell and need my fix, so innocent and distinctive, it falls from her hair, this addictive pheromone caught inside of me leaves me sedated in a virgin lust—a chemical harmony only the two of us could achieve, something so exceedingly precise that it can't be ignored. But her interest lies so fragile. I'll put my idyllic impulses aside for a while to enjoy the moment better.

I still relish that childish summer's blush upon my cheek, and her company fades with it. I'm old enough to realise that matters as such cannot be forced, yet somehow, I've let my emotions run away with me. Those talents I was in awe of and told of her are precisely what impelled her to leave. I'm happy. Well, I should be, shouldn't I? She's been noticed by the company. They've offered her the opportunity to train recruits on a new restaurant opening. Of course, she's gone. I would have done the same, not for the money but for something new, to be put back upon a path of progression.

Self-loathing is what I abandon myself to for whatever I lacked or haven't done. How could I have been so imprudent to run blindly down a path I knew led to nowhere, and now? What is it I've done wrong? Was it that I cared too much? I'm at some fault, and I just don't know what it is, which is what makes it hurt all the more. This sorrow weighs pure within me, and it refuses to leave. It won't happen again. I'll make sure of it. If that means not caring, or not feeling, it's all the same I think. May, where are you, and why aren't you here to help? You know better than me of these matters. Perhaps it's the same hesitation you carried when you came to work at Marty's. Has it made you so distant? And am I now deemed for the same. You told me once that you couldn't love again, and now I've faltered much the same. Where are you, my friends? Think of the conversations we could have had, the things we would have discovered. We led a simple life then. I've read some of the books you loved and spoke of. I guess I never took the time before. I began with that small novel you cherished. I've read it twice already, and it helps. If things don't pick up, I'll probably end up reading his entire works. He understands me, entertains me, like you did. I remember how you came to find him. Stumbling upon him by absolute chance, a fated chance you said. You told me you liked to sit and watch behind the cover of a book in your idle hours, mainly in coffee shops. Not faces or features but mannerisms, mostly movements, and all from the edge of your page. She just enjoyed doing it. With blank expression and shifty stares, you'd see how normal people read, and chatted, or how they sipped their tea and pretended not to look at you. Just mundane things like that. A gentleman nearing the end of his novel, just a few more pages left. You delved into his expression, his fidgeting jaw, feasting thick into the very substance of him. It excited you to see the plot unfold through a flickering glare, she read him as intently as he did his own book, for a matter of minutes until you felt the last page draw near, and that inevitable and excruciating final sentence pass beneath his nose. He shut his eyes and placed the book firmly down on the table. His eyes rested gracefully closed and he spread a crease across his lips of such pleasurable content that she feared he may have momentarily fallen off to sleep, but the pause subsided. A hand swung reassuringly back to the soft cover of the book, and he rocked forward slightly with minimal effort. He placed himself unsteadily to his feet, levelling his oscillating weight with both strained arms. Woefully, a heavy palm was removed, and with a modest shuffle, he took his leave. She had the urge to call out to him, to let him know what he'd done. Knowing May, I can imagine why she couldn't bring herself to do it. She retold every insignificant detail of that scene to me as if reading it from a children's tale, only deliberating on such trivial details as the gentleman's attire and possible nationality. To tell her tale frankly, he'd left the book behind, bound in a red postal band, intentionally she supposed. She had thought about it so much and interpreted his every movement so dramatically that she had come to convince herself that it was left for her. She even described the action of his careless hand parting from his book, as the last thing he held and enjoyed in her presence. She'd wonder why he did it, and whether he did it with all his books, leaving them abandoned to a stranger—an act of utmost reverence to a book and its greater purpose, knowing that if left on a bookshelf, it would only serve to gather dust and yellow. But to be left alone in this unforgiving world, he must have known it would find a way into the right hands. It had chosen her. And after falling in love with it, it had chosen me. 'For you was I born, for you do I have life, for you will I die, for you am I now dying.' We never took the opportunity to speak about it, found it in that book. One of those many things we could discuss for hours. I want to think of it forever and always have remnants of it in my mind. I'll put it on my leg one day, engrain it there forever; it's the only way I'll learn.

———

FRAGMENT 17

We're set to move in soon, myself and Zadie that is. Pangloss had no choice left but to create a new dynamic, so he'd taken her in as a new manager to fill the void. She's been described as a 'go-getter', someone who's going to turn the restaurant upside down and fix all wrongs. At first, he seemed scared to death by the prospect of her arrival, yet diplomatically introduced her as a lady blessed with locks of fiery red, possessing as much spark and vivaciousness as her predecessor. Wild and restlessly ever the centre of a party, not once did I hear her turn down a night out, or a night in for that matter. Drinking in the restaurant's been an almost nightly ritual since the keys to the restaurant came under her safeguard. He thinks it's irresponsible, but truthfully, she's never lost control of her sobriety. Her prior relationship with alcohol must have been exercised to such a point that she no longer felt the benefits of tipsiness; she would often drink past the point of men twice her size, always keeping full charge whether to spur a party on or curbing it if things went too far. She always maintained control. And the more I get to know her, the more there seems to be to her. It's why we get along so well. She's a tricky one to pick flaws in; her maths skills far surpass my own, even with an engineering degree under my belt. In literary circles, she holds authority over all, tearing through novels in a matter of hours. It's her memory that's the key. It binds her and her talents, and it's never aged. Almost as if that lust for learning we all had as a child had never left her; everything was stored in those wide alert pupils of hers to be dispensed at whatever moment she wished. What leaves me aghast and what I now revere the most in her is balance, harmonising positivity and intellect in perfect unison, an uncommon find I've come to gather, and it's that equilibrium I find beautiful. She's the closest of friends, without the complications or the darkness.

Our flat's far from picturesque, the epitome of council block settings in dreary crime-drenched cities, posted high up on the eighth floor of a ceaseless and looming estate; Grangemill's about all we could afford so central. The only aesthetic substance at hand for its construction must have been concrete, or maybe that coarse grey fabric's the only material which has managed to weather the miscreants living within. Our block's one of a family of common towers, the one that's endured the worst of savagery from gangs of children who seethe through corridors like unruly ants, eroding at the structures' innards with smoke and spray cans. The centrum of the great structure comprises of a single lift shaft; nothing of it remains now but a disfigured carcass of its former anatomy. Not so long ago, it'd been burnt beyond recognition, and its stainless-steel walls warp and shine no more. Remnants from the furnace dwell menacingly in the few buttons left inside, melted beyond recognition, rendering the lift incapable. Almost half the floors are out of reach. Those less fortunate than ourselves are loath to take the fire escape stairs from the closest buttoned level to get home. The block is ever-changing. Every day, I salvage something new from the abundance of useless paraphernalia that's discarded in its ageing lift and stairwells. I've tripped over old trumpets and children's undergarments, once even an ash-filled pram, and in time, I've come to treasure these unknown galleries of sorts.

Currently, there's just the five of us at Grangemill, and all from my little chicken shop. Two Brazilian cashiers share the larger double room together, and K and Zadie sleep in the smaller double bed, that just leaves myself in the remaining single room. K's one of those guys whose transient stay in the restaurant had intended to be no more than a part-time job to pay the bills. He's heading for a high-flying consultancy job in the city whilst working as a griller, a surprisingly accomplished one at that. He's one of the quieter ones, as you can imagine—coming straight out of six years' education with an honours in business. I found it hard to fathom what the two of them saw in each other at the beginning. I put it down to an inherent astuteness in them both. But I've realised that their conversations are never just conversations; they're battles, sly digs at the one another's intelligence, useless contestations on worthless facts. Be it capital cities or dates, one would always strive to outwit the other. An outsider to their unique relationship would think they were unhinged, arguing incessantly on such inanities, but they seem quite fond of their ritual.

The time's come, and it's come so soon, too soon. This must be how it feels to be one of those 'if I could be a teen again' people. And all I'm left with now are choices and lots of them, choices and time. Albeit diminishing. And there was me thinking that with age and experience came wisdom; I think I've found that to be untrue a tad too late. A degree and not a clue as to what I should do with it. Life was a lot simpler when I fell into its hands. I should do what everybody else is doing and apply for a job in the city. That would be the simplest option. But beyond the money, I see no benefit, and none of it feels logical to me. Things should be modest, in my thinking, less complicated than the money-motivated nation leads on. People who see it as the 'be all and end all' don't understand that money's solely a tool and in no way definitive of happiness. Not worth sacrificing one's health or youth for that matter. I don't know what I want, but it's not that.

Working full time in the restaurant's keeping me fairly steady, where partying and drinking's become a more natural routine. I've lost count of the times we've drunk the fridges dry. We'd pass clean out, leaving forgotten drinkers sleeping under tables to wake from a nudge or a kick from the first customers of the morning. I dread to think that nothing matters now apart from fleeting hedonism. What's best is each of us knowing how temporal things are, having full appreciation of one another's company. I reckon that's why we enjoy the present so much, knowing that things won't last. The Grangemill era will come to an end with the completion of the contract. The two girls are already planning to head back to Brazil, and then I'm not sure what any of us are going to do. I'm sure things'll fit into place like they always have done.

I feel the word 'lost' is far too diverse and therefore loses a lot in its potency. I want to forget the use of this word in regard to location or cause and think of it essentially as a state of introspective emotion, when one comes to the end of their path and yearns for something, not knowing what. I'm not implying it's a state of desolation, just a purgatorial state of restlessness. I myself am odious to 'lost' in all senses of the word, though I find myself wandering into it all the more as time passes, and my first impulse when feeling its distinct sensation is always to run. Direction matters not when you're lost I suppose.

Paris is just a short journey away, and my knowledge of the language from school is basic to non-existent, which in the whole scale of things, would make it my second language, now that doesn't sound too bad, considering. After all, I've nothing to lose and a lot to learn. So I'll plan of Paris and nothing more, begin by finding a bag big enough and then pack my things, I'll need my skates and some extra clothes, everything else can be binned. Coach is probably the cheapest option but it's a hell of a long journey, and I don't know if I'm coming back. So I suppose it makes no difference how long it takes.

There she was, lying right beside me again, sleeping so heavily and happily just like before. There were no covers above us. Both of us were totally exposed, but warm and secure in our company. I miss the feel of her skin and how it reacted to my touch. With the right pressure and tenderness, my hands sent ripples down her slender beams; soft hairs brushed by fingertips stood erect with delight, swaying in exhaustion as I passed them by. Fingernails played games across her skin, running scantily behind petite ears, around the blemishes that settled on finely drawn neck, then cascading down the channels of her spine, weaving through delicate arches over the sleight of her buttocks, scratching taut skin between her thighs and at the soft nooks behind her knees.

Something had changed. She turned to face the other way and nudged my playful hands away. Drains my lungs of air, causing twitched breath, detest, resentment, it all returns. Rejection had always felt this way. She awoke with a stare that chilled me, an inner loathing intensifies in those eyes of hers that once longed for me. Feelings of then form and dissipate in a moment, and no more do we have the freedom of intimacy; we've become accustomed to it. I was the one at fault and shouldn't have provoked old emotions. What's done is done and can't be untangled or reformed. I know that our emotions are forever to stay in a knot. And this is how we're deemed to go on? Or are we forced to part forever more? Leaving all we built behind us to start again, as destructive as that may be, perhaps it is the only way. She's left. Again I'm alone in the room, the one I slept in as a child, my mother's house after her second separation. I recognise the rustic earthen red walls I'd painted, and the floating shelves I set up as a boy. It's a home but not mine; possibly once it was ours.

I'm up. The kitchen's scented with the puerile light of outdoors, feels like a conservatory. I find myself alone. The dog's water bowl in the corner lies inert and dry, next to it her food bowl. It breathes a story of desperation, of despair. Its steely walls scratched and chewed, and the few food stains left don mouldy hats of emerald. The dog's still here? In intemperance had I lost memory of her, her being, and my responsibilities? How long has she been gone to me? I'm incapable of such injustice. The master bedroom, she must be there, it's where she slept.

And there she lies peacefully on Sister's bed, asleep? Her jet-black fur and yellowed ruff had faded to chalky greys. Health and nutrition's drained, jaunty hip bones protrude and hold up her discoloured coat like a tent. A whimper, she teeters on the edge of existence; can she hear my presence or perhaps a final sigh of relief? I haven't seen her in so long, though her tail rests still. Neglect has committed this, and all I want is to bring her back. I'll cradle her in my arms to feel her trembled breath, gently carry her to the kitchen and attempt to give her light sustenance. Fill her bowl with fresh food and clear water, and watch beside her in anticipation. Time stood steady for just a moment. Faint efforts that lie dormant in her sodden carcass reawaken; she senses her long-anticipated meal and eats, feasting like feral, and drinks so furiously I daren't remove the bowl to refill it. It empties so quick that I can't keep up. I find myself filling glasses full to the brim with water for her to drink, frantically; it's all I do. Time floods sudden with the refilling of water glasses, and with every new glass, I sense her energies replenished. The tall glasses I supply her suffice till her tongue can reach no deeper down crystalline walls, leaving precious inches of water wasted towards the base. My hands won't keep up. Why not add straws to the glasses so she could drink the glass whole? So every glass comes fitted with a straw, and steadily she slurps the entirety of each garnished glass, drying up one after another until sheer gluttonous exhaustion leaves her comatose. Slumped across the stone-tiled floor she lays, saturated in relief; she's safe and happy. I'll join her on the tiles, rest my cold ear on her wheezing chest, and back we fall down into that well of half thought, to the reassuring tune of her heartbeat.

FRAGMENT 18

Didecan knew his journey to Paris would be an arduous one, so he packed the smallest of his belongings into the cushioned liners of his skates, keeping the more cumbersome items of clothing lodged into the unoccupied corners of his oversized carry bag. It was the sturdiest bag he owned and by no standards elegant in any capacity. Shaped by a thin rope lining that joined up in the middle to form a handle, it wrapped itself up tightly in a bright blue tarpaulin skin, visibly scratched and weathered by the more spirited of outdoor elements. He filled it, knowing it would carry the journey, more so than the few items it held.

Knowing that all he possessed was in that sapphire bag of his, he guarded it with all his might. That knack he picked up as a boy for distraction proved invaluable that day, allowing him to sneak the clumsy sack on board past the driver and other passengers who were made to leave their baggage in the undercarriage of the vehicle. He no longer feared inquisition, or assault, or theft. And to his consternation, this element of readiness in the matter happened to deter future happenings.

Each coach came packed to full with holidaying families and furrow-headed commuters. Incessant cries of children echoed, rippling over their riled heads unceasingly from the port of Dover and the farms stretching in between, to their final destination of Paris. For ten wide-awake hours, these captives could hear little but the shrieks of unripe newborn wailing on every aisle, chirping hellishly in a bid to outdo one another like a nest of enraged songbirds. It was unfortunately a one-stop route, which left Didecan and the other passengers at the mercy of these wily cherubs. So he buried his anxieties in literature, amongst the works of many, it was May's books that formed the weightiest constituents of his bag. He bided his time, but grew restless and struggled to pass the time in solitude. Panning his surroundings, he scouted willing passengers to share a friendly word with. The weighty African lady by his side remained out of the question; she was bellowing the entire journey on a miniature mobile phone to someone who sounded like an equally enraged recipient. On top of that, she consumed their entire armrest with almost half of her monstrous arm. To his right, a young lady reading under a dim and narrow glow drew his attention. He watched her for a while, not that her appearance particularly appealed to him, yet for lack of inspiration, he battled amongst thoughts of speaking to her, if only just to jest and pass the time. His gaze lessened and settled in her general direction. And he thought perhaps to elicit conversation would contradict the social regulations that were set on entering the coach. Nobody else interacted or spoke above the bay of children. These sinister constraints forbade its travellers from even looking one another in the eye, let alone conversing. Didecan pondered on how these rules had been imposed on them so naturally and without instruction, whether it was the coach itself that had decided on their conditions or if it was just a vessel for those on board to depict an environment which they preferred to travel in. For there was no policing as to what should or shouldn't be done, and no governing body. Yet the individuals within had apparently chosen to travel in relative isolation. He speculated whether they worried as much as he did about the short periods that passed from one moment to another, or had they ceased trying to squeeze the last drops of appreciation from the present and deliberated that maybe they were unaware the coach had no power over them. Perhaps in their respective worlds outside of the coach, these people felt so condemned to following social expectations that if an opportunity arose for them to create a free life of their own, they might find themselves lost like him. So used to obedience and fitting in they were, but maybe that's all they ever wanted, so he thought perhaps he was the one, the odd one out who wasn't happy or contented and craved for something more?

Her eyes narrowed; she squinted right at him. Didecan was so utterly twisted in thought that he stared straight through her without even realising it and caught a questioning look back. Now he had to say something, anything, to justify his act of discourtesy. Thoughts prophesied an end, and now he was forced to follow. Hastily he stammered an enquiry as to what she read, thinking it impersonal and not too open to ideas of a sexual advance. But then he worried that it could lead her to think he was somewhat of a literary man, which was far from true. It would need some further explanation to get any conversation flowing. Pleasantly they discussed backgrounds, ever an interesting tale to tell, and very soon he managed to grasp an interest. An hour of benign talk went on; he questioned her motives in travelling to Paris, and she confessed she was on her way to an interview for a job in teaching. Politely she asked him the same. Awkwardly he paused, in slow reflective thought of what it may sound like to tell her the truth, so he did, and told her of the absurd position he had put himself in, with no particular detail or flair. She reacted with a puzzled look of disbelief, which swiftly melted to an understanding smirk, a look that implied she had been there once before he thought. Apparently, it was brave of him, a conclusion he would never have arrived to, or agreed with. He had always felt that running away was an act of cowardice, and doubly that a lack of planning was plain reckless. With an uncertain close to the conversation, he thanked her and went back to his reading. Timidly, he felt as absurd as he did before forcing himself to talk, and as much of a stranger in that coach as when he had set off.

They descended into the suburbs of Paris, but it wasn't enough. He longed to see the city centre in all its splendour, and it meant him working out the local metro system. A colour-coded map was sprawled across dusty walls, something familiar. He decided on the ticket machine rather than the cashier, thinking it more forgiving. His foreign coins felt worthless in his palms, too light and too colourful. He imagined he may have been tricked into buying toy money by the Indian lady at the post office. Noticing the crowd gathering behind him, edging in closer at either side, he slid the largest denomination of coin into the machine and waited apprehensively for his change. On board the metro, he felt as at home as he did on the London underground. And he marvelled at how the passenger doors opened with the twist of a handle, at how commuters could speak on their mobile phones inside tunnels, and at the train map that highlighted their path ahead with red dotted bulbs. He received the occasional odd look from travellers, shifty stares at times; it amused him, but no more than the lack of any organised queuing system, or the odd garments he saw others wearing. Nonetheless, he felt safe on their metro regardless of which direction he was heading.

The train continued further into the centre of Paris, and at every stop a few more joined him on his journey. The newcomers brought strange smells, natural scents of vegetation and livestock, market smells for Didecan that compiled and filtered through the carriages of the train. With each station came even more aromas, so foreign and unbearable he needed rid of them, to escape to cleaner airs, and he jumped off at the very next opportunity.

Summer sun struck him sharp, trickling heat through his limbs, and upon his first step, in what he truly felt was Paris, a hollow feeling of pride engulfed him. That hug of warmth lubricated his spirits; the sun's clear rays spelt freedom, feeding his worn muscles and urging him forward through the day. At times, he wondered why he should ever wake if not to wake with the sun upon him. He thought back to his wet city, contemplating how it was he survived so long in such a dark and temperate region. With everything new and alien all around, where he walked was of no consequence, and his only task that day was to find a place of rest for the night. The blue tarpaulin skin bag hung comfortably over his one shoulder, weighing a little more than he cared to remember, so he walked through the unfamiliar streets he was soon to call home, absorbing as much of the environment as he could interpret on the way.

Alike London, multiculturalism wove its way through the entire city, but Paris buzzed a different note; a vibrant flamboyancy rang through its streets and alleyways. Pavements were far wider than he ever became used to; they encouraged people to meander through the expansive avenues, rather than brisk and linear like he would. The luminescence of the new city slowed his pace. Soaring Gothic structures reflected high over the heart of town drizzling a climate of tainted romance into the streets below. Local inhabitants borne of this exuberance sold golden trinkets off petite rugs and handcrafted stalls all around him. He walked on for as far as it took for his settings to change, till he ambled upon the reconstructed district of St-Michel. Rapscallion men stood at every corner, and Didecan mistrusted the looks of them all, especially the rowdier ones swarming at the burrows of metro station exits, bellowing their trade. One of them caught his eye, setting off towards him, muttering French inanities. He attempted to discourage the noisy man, but it came to no avail and instantaneously he realised his proficiency in French had come to nil. Sensing an Englishman, the lout eloquently offered Didecan a haircut for ten euros. He declined embarrassedly and marched on. The grand city fell heavy on his shoulders, and the blue bag he had wielded for so long left blisters on his palms. On a nearby bench, he sought some respite to regain his breath. Nothing he had packed with him could help satiate the bruises on his palms, and with no way of telling where the nearest pharmacy could be, he worried that even if he found the proper outlet, he would have no way of asking for what it was he actually wanted.

In the event he couldn't find a room for the night, Didecan spied a grotty alcove underneath the arches of an overground station that guaranteed shelter from the elements. It had sure signs of being slept in and would serve as a sound back-up if not already occupied on his return. He knew, however, he could rely on the help of two old acquaintances who might assist him. The handful of money he took with him would only stretch for a few weeks at best without work, which would carry even further if he managed to stay with one of his contacts in Paris, just until he settled.

The young man Barnabas stood as his first calling. He had an aunt in London that he visited infrequently, who served as the perfect pretext to leave his hometown and skate in the city. The two met on London's streets, and Barnabas consequently became an honorary member of the crew any time he visited. Conversations were limited to schoolroom basics, and as Didecan came to discover soon after, his French spattered with hip hop nourished street slang and African nuances. All Didecan knew was that he lived in the 'banlieues' with his family and worked occasionally in his father's Nigerian restaurant by which they prospered. Barnabas battled against both his father and education, following a lifestyle dedicated to hip hop and skating; thus he retained knowledge of the Parisian streets comparable to Didecan's grasp of his own pavements. He was assured that his friend would return the favour and greet him with open arms or even just a bed for a few nights, so he extracted his number from the back of a scrawled-up old note he had sketched up before leaving. After a few fumbled attempts deciphering the foreign extension system, he got through on the third attempt, and to his ecstasy, Barnabas was thrilled to hear of his presence in town. They arranged to meet a few hours later for a short skate at the world-renowned Bercy ledges, used primarily as a sporting stadium and venue for legendary concerts, but it held no further interest to skaters outside its unique form and thickly waxed ledges. The thought of setting foot upon its hallowed ground thrilled Didecan, even more so than the prospect of having a bed for the night.

Barnabas's family stayed so far outside of the city centre that he felt it impractical to find work so soon and maintained that having to commute every day would be a waste of his time. Instead, they skated each day, mingling in different districts till spent, and arriving to the family house for dinner on the table and freshly starched bed sheets. They treated him like their own, providing him with food and shelter regardless of the obvious divide in language. He often thought this ill communication was precisely what fed Barnabas's mother's maternal fondness for him and further implicated him as the child of the house. And over the weeks, he ate up the morsels of French language left to him by the mother, who always lent an ear to Didecan's babble while busying herself in the house with chores or cooking. Strangely enough, he found the home far messier than he was ever used to living in, and he spent most of his time indoors tidying the anthills of butter and crumbs that gathered through the house. His behaviour absolutely astounded the mother, and impelled her to regard him as something of an aged sort of child.

As well treated as he was in that household, he still felt compelled to leave and willed to regain his independence with a flat and a key of his very own. He grew weary of relying on someone to enter, or making arrangements to be driven to the closest train station any time he had the urge to wander the city. His movements steadily traced Barnabas's just to make leaving the house easier; appreciative as he was, he could never grow accustomed to that feeling of indebtedness that came with having his fanciful freedoms taken. Graciously he thanked the family in whatever form or French came readily and left for the centre of town.

FRAGMENT 19

In a slightly better known city he called upon his final contact Momo. She was an old colleague of his from the chicken shop, who spent more of her time socialising with the team outside of work than he remembered her actually working. Most presumed she had only acquired a job in London to meet friends and drinking partners. Her looks reflected the lifestyle she led absolutely, an excessive socialite whose natural good figure came marred by a concoction of sleep deprivation, alcohol, and drugs. Didecan was not often one to call in favours, but his case proved a matter of necessity, and it felt all the worse that he hadn't maintained any contact with her since she had left for Paris a year earlier. Nevertheless, he tried his luck.

Their short telephone conversation delivered him to a settlement of tower blocks much like a rejuvenated form of his dearly missed Grangemill. Her apartment hung high above the crumbling district. Looking around the estate, he felt surrounded by a youth he felt no bond with and chuckled at the sight of the angry-looking yobs parading on street corners—just overgrown boys on miniature bikes, wearing garish hip hop clothing draped on lean torsos. Outside of the pack culture that every modern city nourishes, Parisian ghettos appeared to nurture a depraved generation of youth, donning the whitest of trainers and driest lips of bleeding red. He watched them drink wine from the bottle and spend their daylight hours in hoods, scanning pavements for cigarette remnants. They screwed faces of ferocity that bemused him, even more, that none had the audacity to approach or accost him. A facade, he mused; possibly it made their conditions survivable.

He rapped eagerly at the door, wondering if with just a faded memory of her outline he would recognise any changes in her, but the door opened out on him before he had a chance to muster his thoughts. And there she stood. Floppy auburn hair spread neatly across her petite shoulders covering faded olive skin. A quintessentially French look, he thought. Once more he was disappointed to find that she was as much a slave to marijuana as he had remembered from before. Its earthy scent crept past him as he entered. He often debated as to how easy-going she would have been without it, or if that was a value inherent in her. The apartment was hers, a hand-me-down from a divorced father, and the only factor that kept both her and her mother in Paris. The mother, whose name he could never recall, popped into the flat at whatever day took her fancy, with neither him nor Momo having any knowledge of her whereabouts on other days. He woke to the coarse fragrance of fresh brewed coffee, and knew that her mother was home when it wafted at its strongest. Caffeine seemed to be all she ever came back to the house for, and in need of nothing more to occupy her time, she moved within the house, living a life of simple routines and pleasures. French was all that she spoke; it came intermittently in sporadic bursts of shrill complacency that were only ever directed at Momo since she never took the initiative to speak directly to Didecan, and in turn, he behaved with her in much the same approach.

Momo's relaxed demeanour made it impossible for him to feel he was imposing in any way, and her generosity extended to assisting another German acquaintance with her bed to share for a month's stay. He was uncertain as to whether Momo declined any requests; the last thing he would have wanted to do was capitalise on her good nature, yet at the back of his mind he knew that at some point she would have to learn to say no, if not taught by him, then undoubtedly by someone else. The arrival of the German girl wreaked havoc in their small household. Shy and uncertain in character, she encased herself in an overgrown body of childish proportions, an anomaly to the core. Didecan's interactions with her would spiral into charitable tales of self-loathing, he regarded her behaviour as simply an attention-seeking habit and did his best to avoid her. But the flat was just too small to provide him any peace, and at every opportunity, she clung to his arm like a limpet. Her close presence made him physically uncomfortable, though he was sure that by keeping her company he was somehow making Momo's life at home a little easier, at least for the while.

Nights spent alongside Momo and her friends were mostly in the heart of town, charming their ways into niche bars on Le Champs Elysees, sipping on tall cocktails, or often at heated house parties, deep-set in the crudest of city lodgings. These drug-fuelled parties left Didecan feeling shunned and morose, and his unwillingness to partake in their debauched activities left doubt in his reasons for ever being there. The German girl, however, thrived at these parties. She seemed to have found a comfortable setting to talk with others in a mutually disorientated state. He watched on as her sociability peaked, taking carefully measured concoctions of drug that allowed her to be who she wanted to be. He contemplated that it might be a matter of her subconscious knowing that nothing she said mattered at the time and would surely be forgotten the next day that gave her that sense of liberation. In Momo's flat, he felt somehow responsible for her; even in that intoxicated state, he found her unbearable. At the last party he had escorted her to, he discovered her trapped in an empty bedroom, clamouring that she was forced into an uncompromising ménage à trois among an amorous French duo. He was certain the whole ordeal was through no one's fault but her own, if indeed it did occur, and chose to indulge her no more. He marched her back to Momo's and ceased to attend those parties any more.

The guilt of staying rent-free at Momo's compiled with the extra weight of the German pressed him to leave, but before that he required a steady income. He went on the lookout for work of any kind. As was his preference, he went door to door; however, in the strange environment he trawled, he found there was no use for a man speaking so little of the native tongue. He searched in bars and restaurants throughout the busier districts, but holding conversations past initial introductions proved to be more difficult than he had expected. A full day of rejections dissolved his prospects of staying in the city much longer, though he persevered blindly, and with the next day, came a new strategy. Thinking his fluency in English might benefit him in certain trade, his next tactic targeted touristic venues where his English skills might be an asset. A few attempts at employment in hostels took him to a third in Jaures, a watery district split in population by French-Algerians and travellers. Momo forewarned him of such areas where criminal notoriety bred from the poverty that surrounded. She told him that looking there would be risky, but he saw no other options.

The directions he was given were simple, yet the hostel eluded him. Every route took him to the same dodgy-looking bar, whichever way he tried to go about finding it. On enquiring within the pokey bar, he found that spare rooms lay hidden above, spread over six exceedingly narrow floors. Naturally he befriended the staff, then followed with innocent inquisitions on work, which summoned him to a broad wooden table at the far end of the bar, where an enormous sun-blushed lady sat in wait for him. She was an American through and through, jolly and exuberant. He tried his utmost to reciprocate her excitement, hoping it would land him a job, but he was thrown when it transpired that she worked illegally at the hostel providing local tours for guests. She lived under the radar with her French partner, just outside of the city, and was looking to expand her illegitimate business. And if Didecan were up to scratch, he might assist in running her tours. She informed him there would be an element of training required where he could make a little money. Another prospect for him might be the night shift job, which she described as being paid to sleep, and it pained her to admit, that he might be interrupted every so often by drunken guests who had to be let back inside.

He spent weeks shadowing the bubbly American as she cajoled late-night drinkers into joining the morning tours, and earned him ten Euros a punter. He dissected her techniques in motivating the group, studying her body language and charms that every tour group craved, extracting the best parts of her work, in preparation for one day taking tours of his very own. He concluded that repetition was her downfall. Every week he heard the same puns on tour and the very same spontaneous laughter from both herself and her willing audience. It upset him that she had become so accustomed to her work, rigging it with faked impulsiveness, knowing that every day drew a different crowd who knew no better. Didecan envisaged his own tour to be bespoke; he wanted every tour a distinct product of the group, with individual pace and style matching the dynamics of the people. And his opportunity came sooner than expected, when just two weeks on he was given the graveyard tour of Père Lachaise to run, as well as working the sleep shift at the hostel.

His working day would start past midnight. On his arrival to the hostel, a beer was always thrust upon him at the bar from Erwin, the disagreeable closing barman. The beer always came accompanied with a demand for some amount of money; Didecan loathed him from the very beginning. This signalled the start of his shift and was the moment he needed to be at his most vigilant, for work began at the first sip and important decisions had to be made on whom to coax at a full bar of travellers. He thought of where best to ply his trade, when every tourist required a different tactic. One option he adopted for the organised-looking tourist was the upfront approach. These types were the easiest to tell apart by their flurry of brochures, and were also the quickest to get on board. He'd join the group as the official representative of the hostel, offering tours for the next morning, and give a comprehensive explanation of the benefits they could reap from coming on the tour. Weighing up the benefits of his, rather than the plethora of other tours around town, this analytical approach brought reliable clientele by the droves. However, these sorts did nothing to build group amity. His preferred technique guaranteed a lively dynamic for the tour; and it only ever worked for the more animated and outgoing drinkers. He simply joined them as a fellow fun seeker, won their interest and affection, and then popped in the tour as a suggestion. It got them drunk and sprightly even before the tour had begun, and was a sure-fire way of making friends and business.

The bar closed at two. He bade Erwin and his guests farewell, escorting the drunkards off the premises, and continued closing down the bar for the night. Disputes with French regulars would often stem from his shortcomings in the language and were often used as an opportunity for them to stay a while longer, but a little force was all he needed to have the front door locked, and the bar to himself.

He'd sweep the floor, then follow with a mop, and promptly set his weary mind on rest. Perpetual humming from illuminated fridges behind the bar were the only assuring sounds that kept him company whilst he constructed his bed. Out of bar stools and bed sheets he built a fortress, a tent of linen that ensured his privacy. Every night he spent on the bar floor went in a semi-conscious daze. Seldom would a siren or a passing drunk stir his light slumber, a potential guest perhaps, arriving late from a club in the early hours, or an unruly drunkard demanding one more. A couple of hours' sleep was all he was permitted before an eight o'clock-start, just in time for the first batch of croissants at the bakery next door.

—

The much-anticipated tour hailed the long-awaited last stretch of his working day, and by nine sharp, all the tour goers would gather at the bar to set off. He had learnt by heart all the facts for the tour and added to them nightly; since every group had a different zeal, he found himself constantly adapting and finding new ways to entertain his group. Five metro stops took them to the infamous cemetery of Père Lachaise. Spanning over one hundred acres and housing some of the world's greatest decaying remains, though its historical significance was not but a scratch on that of the inhabitants who rest dormant within. In an area with such macabre purpose, life burst from every crevice. Swept gravel pathways, fortified teams of prying school children, and, in the darkest of corners, rich green shoots spouted out from the fertile brilliance of those who rest beneath. The cemetery had an almost supernatural feeling to it. A lost city overflowing with crumbling tombs and dark chasms, it was a land he could have discovered as a child had he ever grown up in Paris, and as an adult it was his duty to lead eager pleasure-seekers in his wake. In time, he came to understand the labyrinth in its entirety. A single tree stump or odd rock would guide him to a site of importance, and marching moments in between were filled with laughter. Their journey uncovered the venerable corpses of Frédéric Chopin, Jim Morrison, and Oscar Wilde. It took them along broad asphalt pathways built for the crowds and more often than not, down narrow weed-restricted paths or steep rocky short cuts which sent them swiftly to new sections of the cemetery. In two short hours, he covered the most reputable and mysterious of attractions; then he took them out of the cemetery borders, back into the old world where they lived not such a long time ago. They dribbled down the hilly slopes, through rickety street markets that cluttered with oddly acquired artefacts and delicate Eastern silks, gently down towards the manufactured Parc des Buttes Chaumont. The walk would exhaust many of the less agile members, so he made sure to grant them all respite at one of the dainty roadside cafes en route. Late July was arid and bright, the hottest that Paris had to give and the height of travel season. Didecan's beige skin turned to dark caramel amidst a sea of blistered red travellers; sunshine caressed his skin and kept him perfectly at ease. His spirits lifted, and thoughts of home came to nothing but a discoloured memory.

Before continuing their journey, he made a call back to the American lady at the hostel, instructing her to commence with the next part of the tour. As they pattered through endless alleys mosaicked with intricate carpets, they marvelled at the ornaments which had gathered from the world over; then they came to a hill. It stood grand enough to be spotted from a mile away, yet the path they distractedly ambled upon allowed the hill to creep up on them. The incline was steep, and each tiny yellowed brick step that split down the middle stood barely wide enough for one's full toe to fit. They were made to toil in order to reach the next stage. He absolutely forbade rest after the cafe, and urged them upwards. At three-quarters of the summit, alveoli-like feather-topped trees emerged faintly from beyond the last stair, pinnacles that guided them safely to a formulated paradise, a synthetic Eden. Within the park's broad golden gates, they could oversee the full scale of the gardens unfold before them, expanding in altitude as far as in breadth. Jagged rock waterfalls governed the park from high, feeding life downwards in subtle streams that wove between frolicsome dogs and children and ended in a still pool tens of metres beneath their feet. In juxtaposed urbanity, one could feel unnatural looking upon lush landscapes engraved amidst such Gothic backdrops; it left Didecan and his followers awe-eyed every week they journeyed forth.

Meandering through leafy *terroir* bordering lakes and waterfalls, sprinting past sprinklers, he marched his faithful troop through an orchestrated forest until they reached a large clearing in the grass. A single blue cotton sheet carpeted the central patch, spread out for them by the caring hands of the American lady who had prepared plates of local cheese and Beaujolais for the fatigued tour goers, bringing their day to a subtle close. He would often stay silent at this point, American lady at his side, and observe. His work was complete, and it amazed him how little time it took to assemble a group of friends. He reflected back to the morning, serving coffees, overhearing their fumbled conversations, and it pleased him to think that he had played a part in it, in creating something so intangible. Back at the hostel they divided their share of the takings, and both went their separate ways.

Bercy stadium was where Didecan began his session, in a small rusted skatepark that hid sheltered behind the sloping jade-faced lawns of Le Palais de Omnisports. He approached, already spent, shuffling skates in hand along sandy straights. He first found himself drawn there from the noise and clatter of scrapes from fervent skaters that echoed off the steel enclosure. Dense shrubbery had clothed the eyesore, which hid in the shadow of the great grass pyramid, yet it retained an essence of dignity about it, a certain dusty beauty aside its violent sprayed multicolour surfaces—some gritty persona, polluted and exemplified by the rebellious youth who skated its rigid framework. Regulars at the park swilled wine from daybreak; cigarette-puffing youths pulsed broodily through skaters that donned sunglasses and hoods come rain or shine. To his good fortune, these petty criminals held skating in the highest regard, and his proficiency in the art kept him out of trouble for his time there. It was from these self-impoverished adolescents that he picked up the more complex aspects of the local language, and their patience and perseverance allowed him to flourish.

FRAGMENT 20

In these fruitful times, Didecan stumbled across a chance lifeline, from perhaps the last place he would care to lend help. A tip-off from a learned traveller took him to the wealthier districts of the city that formed along the banks of La Seine—a district where pavements stretched wider than roads, where young well-to-do Parisians might raise a family free from crime and poverty and hardship. The building he sought looked over the slowest flowing parts of the river. 'The American Church' he was told, grew fat with moss and moisture, and held hope for him in finding a place to set down his bag and call home. A famed wall concealed within one of its many distinguished courtyards was reputed to hold the key for cheap accommodation, owned and rented out by neighbouring churchgoers. Through these antiquated means Didecan had uncovered the details of an old Frenchman by the name of Jacques, who sought to let his apartment for a few months whilst out of town. His small house balanced neatly upon the rustic pebble paths of hilly Montmartre, possibly the quaintest little area of Paris near untouched by time and contemporary architecture, laced with charming boutiques and rickety cottages. The apartment was perfectly situated in between Le Sacré Coeur, towering gracefully at the tip of the mount overlooking the city, and the lowest part of Pigalle, known for its seedy sex districts and the infamous Moulin Rouge. Every aspect of Montmartre rattled legend and adventure, from the Dutch windmills that near toppled on brick slopes, to the house itself that Didecan went to visit.

He was informed that the apartment could only be reached on foot from the station via countless stone pathways and lamp-lit stair sets. Jacques welcomed a perspiring Didecan at the door with a handshake and black coffee. He was of the smallest proportions, a quality of old age Didecan presumed—which also explained his worn clothes and overall grey appearance, as well as attributing the house with his soft musky odour. The animated man chose to soak his house in shadow. Bulbs in every room shone jaundiced with age-old dust; it allowed a mist of barely visible clutter to surround them. Strange structures modelled from narrow steel rods and foam spheres furnished every shelf and free crevice of the house. They exchanged pleasantries in the living room, which doubled as Jacques' bedroom by use of a bunk bed stuffed into one end. After polite introductions, Didecan discovered they shared a common engineering background. He questioned the old man a little using the limited French he could gather to investigate the matter of the tiny structures that invaded his house; his reply could easily have been mistaken for the ramblings of a madman if not for their immediate setting, which in some way made his explanations all the more plausible. Tentatively, Jacques confessed to having headed a government-funded research facility further up the hill, and uncovered the molecular objects dotted around the house to be vital components in his work. A mood of solemnity came over Jacques, and with an amount of consternation, he continued to disclose that his project had been recently terminated and funding was ceased. The science behind this unsettled man's theories fascinated Didecan. Jacques believed truly to have been on the trail to forming a vital link between nature and certain sacred scripture. Through complex logarithms, he forged a path derived by the formulation of patterns in leaves. His unnerving eagerness had driven him to spread his findings in the world; it had even permitted him to regard Didecan as a fellow scientist. He lectured him through his greatest findings, heralding three-dimensional graphs he had believed early philosophers and mathematicians to have developed, and consequently utilised to produce the timeless texts that have shaped religion, creating order in a society of disorder. He envisaged his discovery would change the civilised world as he knew it, till the Government contravened to stop his team from unearthing any conclusive evidence. The techniques Jacques had called upon far outstretched Didecan's mathematical comprehension, yet the method he had used to derive such potent conclusions appeared methodical. Little did he know it, but his understanding of Jaques's research came along with the trust and safekeeping of his house and, more importantly, his work.

He gave him the keys that very day on one condition, which further mystified his aberration and encroached on Didecan's privacy. Jaques delivered a forewarning that from time to time the house may be breached by an acquaintance of his whom also held a copy of the keys, but he reassured Didecan that the man was a harmless artist who worked at the top of the hill painting caricatures. Having no permanent home of his own, he visited now and again, spending the night and departing well before morning broke. Didecan worried little since he had nothing much of worth with him, and only ever planned to spend a few hours sleeping at the house before starting work. He heartily agreed and set his bag down in Jacques's bedroom to rest for a while. During Didecan's stay at the house, not once did he set eyes upon the ageing artist, though he could sense from the muddled misalignment of microstructures in the common areas of the house and unfamiliar scents that lingered in the afternoon when he had made himself welcome.

Having a house of his own and work that he enjoyed made Didecan really feel a part of his new life. Skating had never been simpler with a spot like Bercy close by. It was perpetually brimming with skaters, so nothing needed to be planned. There was always a friendly face to greet him or a group of touring Europeans keen to journey with him to distant parts of the city. His most entertaining sessions were always with newcomers to the city hunting adventure and novel street architecture, unlike the Parisian locals, who had grown spoilt by their city's luxuriance and ambled no further than the outskirts of Bercy.

The long days left him weary and satisfied. Consuming lethargy kept his mind at ease and thoughts of wanting more—a luxury of the work-shy. Just two complications threatened his idyll. First was that impending moment when in just a few months his picturesque house in Montmartre would be taken once Jacques returned, and the second concerned his wavering relations with the closing barmen at the hostel.

Erwin was a brute born and raised in the pits of East London and dropped into the outskirts of Paris by his late father. As a child he began his slow descent into drug abuse and alcohol addiction, and soon developed a violent streak to match. On arrival to the city, his father made sure to arm him with all the French he needed to permeate the Parisian drug scene and carry favour with the local Algerian gangs in Jaures to form a reputation in the district. Those attributes suited their location adequately, and just in case, a precautionary canister of mace and a well-worn baseball bat was kept beneath the counter if trouble caught up to him. Their disagreements began from Didecan's very first day at work. He just couldn't fathom the spiteful way Erwin spoke to others and Didecan too came to be ridiculed over his accent. Seeing him unaffected, Erwin escalated his coercions to threats of violence. The outbursts took Didecan off guard and he brushed them off as outlandish drunken banter, but his behaviour only seemed to worsen by Didecan's nonchalance to the provocation. With only the two of them working almost every night, Erwin became an ineluctable burden. Didecan had witnessed the most heinous atrocities Erwin could conjure, and beside each horror came barbaric guarantees if he were to respond. Night shifts tormented him, though Erwin's volatility cautioned him to thinking twice about confronting the man he feared and despised for the simple risk of losing his job.

The moment came one evening. Threatened by the threadbare baseball bat stashed behind the counter, Didecan parried that he had tired of hearing empty threats night after night and willed Erwin to act on his will. Erwin's first fiendish instinct was to drive a fist into Didecan's jaw, which he narrowly dodged. He took the inebriated beast by the shirt, propelling him spine first into the tills. A tussle ensued with knees and jabs for just a few seconds until loyal drinkers tore them apart and kicked Erwin out of the bar, shamed and bloody. A sense of duty took over, and Didecan began his usual routine of locking the doors to shut down the hostel early for the night. He hoped to stay there in safety, till the morning at least. The entire night he dwelled on what Erwin might do to him, fearing he might return with a knife. He'd once heard that Erwin had used a screwdriver on a local dealer; if anything was certain, he knew Erwin would seek to exact revenge in some way. So what good would reason do? For lack of a better solution, he made a call to the owner, demanding to meet him before taking the last of his tour groups through Paris. Wide awake, he waited and thought of nothing. In that moment, all was still and he felt all was not lost. That was a feeling that reassured him. In all his time, it was the first that he had managed to pass the moment in unthinking tranquillity, and he treasured it. He looked to the ceiling and felt his surroundings brighter every second. A warm sun rose to his surprise, the beginning of a brand new era, a new day, and a brand new feeling. And he wondered precisely when it was that it happened, when every morning felt much the same. It eluded him. He could certainly remember back to when his mornings felt brand new.

A business-like figure dressed in a neatly pressed suit appeared punctually the next morning. Didecan thought it hard to believe that this busy suit of a man could own such an underhand establishment. He sensed that he didn't often make house calls, and it was made clear to him that he had a lot more under his care than Didecan's tiny old hostel, which must have made him little to no money. The owner knew nothing of the intricacies or goings-on inside his hostel and had absolutely no knowledge of his presence there for the last three months. Despite his efforts in retelling of the previous night's events, the owner remained impervious to the thought of confronting Erwin, and all too soon it became obvious that the owner had written off any efforts in managing him or the hostel a long time ago and he remained content to let the business run itself as long as it made some profit. Erwin, an inexorable prince, would continue to rule as he wished in that runaway district, an unfortunate outcome for both Didecan and the hostel owner. Didecan cordially thanked the owner for his time and departed, fearing what wickedness Erwin might impose on his return.

Didecan made preparations to return the flat to Jacques. His pride prevented him from asking of any more, be it for shelter or for money. And each day that passed, looking for a home toughened with ever-dwindling funds. Occasionally, he was turned away from lodgings on sight, and often without reason; before long, the week was up and he still remained desperately in want of a place to call home. He bid Jacques a final adieu, who kindly welcomed him to stay on a little if he needed, but he proceeded to pack his bag full, noticing that he had a lot more room in there than he had previously remembered. Everything fit in snugly—there was even a little space for food. He took a final look around the house to find anything he may have left behind, and he found nothing, then went to wander.

Time was of no consequence. He had no work and no place to go. So he walked, unlike he had done so before in that splendid city, rambling listlessly through memorable avenues, tracing through criss-crossed streets, this time to the American church which held his last thread of hope in unearthing a house for himself. On his arrival to the fabled church, he witnessed that fateful wall blank. There were no letters or even a notice tied up to it like before, not even a pin mark or scrap of blue tack, and the wet green mould that clung to the brick wall seemed untouched. He brushed the wall with one hand, and the green substance spread to his dry fingertips. Fatigued from the walk and absolute futility of his efforts, he decided to take rest on a shallow wooden bench just outside the church, overlooking the broad river. La Seine ebbed viscous, motionlessly back and forth. He observed the passers-by and dog walkers fleeting past without a second thought, like the water before him, and the slow growth of movement around. Making use of the moment, he chiselled his name lightly into the brittle green varnish that protected his bench and fell soft asleep, clutching the corners of a plastic sapphire bag over a cold ear.

He took advantage of that bench for a while, interrupting sleep and contemplation with travel to the city. He read to the furthest ends of metro lines and darted to Bercy for impromptu sessions during the day, sauntering through unexplored parts of the city till the sun set in. He'd meander back to the river and find that bench to lie on, and shut his eyes and listen, to the grumbling of metro trains passing peacefully below him through the night.

3864344R00073

Printed in Great Britain
by Amazon.co.uk, Ltd.,
Marston Gate.